EXPLORING IRRESISTIBLE
new uncut edition

ANASTASIA AMOR

BRODT PUBLISHING

BRODT PUBLISHING
EXPLORING IRRESISTIBLE
new uncut edition
AnastasiaAmor.com
Copyright © 2008 by Anna Brodt
All rights reserved.
ISBN:9780992134327
Cover art by Anna Brodt
Author photo by Kristen Wells

EXPLORING IRRESISTIBLE...erotic romance...5 stars!

"Exploring Irresistible is as decadent as fine dark chocolate and tropical drinks. Amor's vivid descriptions put me right there. What I love best is that I can come back and enjoy this story over and over again. This book is sensuous romance at its best. Hot sultry Puerto Rico. When Aleese sees sinfully irresistible Arman—a man like chocolate...the tiger inside her is unleashed! A fight for control over her life surges into a burning adventure of passion and erotic fantasy...
Irresistible in every way!"—*Michelle Stinson Ross*

1

Freedom.

Aleese had escaped the confines of her hotel room and was sitting in an outdoor café facing the square, a balmy breeze fanning her face. Whatever Keith was doing no longer concerned her. She was only glad she had the morning to herself away from him. After working her way up and down the hilly cobblestone streets of San Juan, she had decided to take a rest and enjoy the sun before the inevitable return to the hotel, and to Keith.

Sipping a steamy hot coffee, she bit into a flaky chocolate croissant—letting go of the tension in her shoulders. Rich, decadent chocolate brushed her tongue and as she brought it up to the roof of her mouth, Aleese held it there. No, she wouldn't swallow it—she'd leave it, letting the sinful flavor in light buttery pastry pleasure her senses. Endorphins delightfully bounced in her brain, elevating her into a state of euphoria. Yet, she still needed to keep the captured sinful cocoa prisoner. But it was out of her control. No matter how much she willed it to stay, her mouth watered with the delicious, thickness, enticing her to savor it until there was no choice. Aleese swallowed the chocolate nectar.

Closing her eyes, she let the marvelous liquid glide down. As her eyes opened, Aleese's gaze fell upon a dark-haired stranger casually dressed in jeans and white shirt striding towards a nearby table.

From her proximity to his table, Aleese could observe him unnoticed as he sat down. His unruly, black hair brushed his collar. The white cotton shirt did nothing to disguise the powerfully built shoulders and forearms—so unlike Keith. Her eyes trailed down the length of his long denim-clad legs, stretched out as he leaned back in his chair. Picking up a newspaper left behind by another patron, he started reading just as the waiter returned with a coffee, as if already knowing what the stranger wanted.

He drank it black. Keith liked his with thick cream and lots of sugar, which reminded Aleese he hated to be kept waiting. Keith would get that look on his face, purse his lips and say something pompous. From out of her wallet, Aleese dug up some coins and tossed them on the table, all the while wishing she could see the stranger's eyes. Tracing her finger along the curve of her lips she stared at that sensuous mouth. The handsome stranger glanced up from the newspaper. Was he looking back? It was too hard to tell with those mirrored shades. His eyes were a secret, as were her own.

Outside clouds covered the sun. Aleese took off her sunglasses and stood up. On her way out she edged to the exit still holding on to her sunglasses, undecided as to wear them or not. At the last minute, she turned and looked back at the man. He, too, had removed his sunglasses. Dark smoldering eyes met hers—burning a hole in her body.

* * * *

In the hotel room, Aleese lay on the bed resting, imagining the sexy stranger. From the bathroom, water rushed rhythmically. Keith was taking a shower.

Tugging a purple lipstick-like object from her purse, she placed it on the bed. The thin cotton of her spaghetti top easily pushed down as her hand smoothed over the rise of her breast. Fingertips curved around forcing the soft mound out of the push-up bra. Funny how her left nipple always seemed erect, even without gently manipulating it. With one hand, she cupped a breast, while the other stroked and teased a nipple.

The stranger appeared on the bed. He brought his mouth to the eager peak and sucked it—drawing it in and releasing it ever so slightly until it was gripped tightly once again between full sensuous lips.

That tingle between Aleese's legs grew stronger, but she ignored it, shoving the top down allowing free access to the other breast. But the material kept creeping back. Impatiently, Aleese jerked the straps down. Her breasts would be his. The stranger straddled her, stroking and playing until her nipples swelled and hardened. And of course, he wanted more.

Aleese listened for signs of activity from the bathroom. The water was still running steadily. She had time, yet precious little of it.

Pushing her skirt up, she poked her finger under her panties, gliding down over her soft skin to the moist opening below. Arousal had made her wet. Lifting the edge of the lacy panties, she dipped the end of the purple toy down into the sticky nectar gathered there.

Aleese had only one plaything, which she had boldly ordered on the internet. Too shy to go into the local novelty shop and ask for a clitoral vibrator she had gone all out and bought this little miracle maker along with some sensational lube that delivered ecstasy in a bottle. No one would ever have expected this little lipstick to be a mechanism for pleasure. In combination with the lube she always reached a mind-blowing orgasm.

Uptight Keith never suspected she had such a thing. Middleclass, from a conservative family, not to mention having a massive ego—he'd find the whole thing offensive. Why would any woman need a vibrator if he, the stud machine, was around to fuck her?

Before she switched it on she coated the tip with a silky lube. The pheromones gave it a sweet scent. Switching the pliable toy on, she pressed the button until the strongest pulsing sensation vibrated. One hand dove under her mini skirt while the other pulled her panties slightly down to allow the magic to press against her clit. Rolling onto her side, Aleese jerked the panties lower over the curve of her butt and gripped a cheek. How she wished a third hand was there to stroke both breasts and nipples.

Fantasizing dark hair falling over her mounds, she pictured full lips sucking a nipple. Urgently, he reached around and pushed the vibrator away. Substituting a finger, he slid it up and down over the soft folds. She squirmed with pleasure as her imaginary lover, sensing her need, brought his mouth down.

Her clit pulsed with the beat of the vibrator and she imagined a thick, strong rod entering her. The stranger fucked her so hard she—Aleese contracted her pussy and groaned loudly as the sensation surged to a new height. She was almost there. Sweat filmed under her arms and her juices flowed. Tightening her thighs, she struggled to keep the toy on her aching nub. Aleese needed to retain the tension to reach orgasm. Images whirled in her brain. Fire ignited in her core. Shuddering, the intense vibes pushed her over the edge. With a scream, Aleese came.

The water turned off in the bathroom. "You okay?"

"Just bumped the bed," she managed to reply. Fighting the urge to just lay there enjoying the aftermath of the orgasm, Aleese hastily covered up and quickly tossed the magic lipstick into her tote bag.

Keith had been oblivious to her leaving—that was the way he was with everything. He was a Brit. Intelligent, cool and calculating. That wasn't the bad part. It was the engineer part that irked her.

A few months back, when they'd first met, she'd been impressed. Only a year older, Keith already owned a house and a BMW, while she rented a condo and paid a car loan. First year teachers didn't earn much in Canada. Owning a house would be a long time coming.

At first, Aleese had been happy. With the beginning of winter, Keith was eager to learn to ski. How romantic to be in the snow together on a sunny day. She volunteered to teach him but instead of appreciating this, he went on and on about how good he was. In fact, he was a natural. His first day skiing was so much better than her three years of practice. It was macho BS, but nevertheless, it hurt. It made her doubt her decision to stick it out in a relationship with a man. But there had been too many boyfriends—none of them right. Six months with Keith was coming up and she wanted to prove to herself she wasn't flighty, with no substance.

"Hey, clumsy! What happened?"

"Bumped the bed with my knee."

A towel wrapped around his waist, Keith made his way over to the bed. The room had two double beds and she'd made the one closest to the window hers. "Bought shoes, I'd bet."

Aleese glanced at her tote bag, containing a packaged gold metallic bikini. "Nope. No shoes. What about you?"

Keith lay down on the bed beside her, his arm draped over her hip. "Talked to a few boat owners," he said, before lowering himself on the bed.

Before he could kiss her, Aleese blurted out, "I've got a headache, Keith."

Bringing his face closer, he said soothingly, "You'll be fine. Relax. You're just not used to the sun and the heat of the tropics."

He kissed Aleese, thrusting his tongue in between her teeth—flicking it in and out. Aleese lay passively, accepting his lizard-like thrusts. Neither resisting nor participating, she zoned out. Keith seemed oblivious of her lack of enthusiasm. He lingered, unlike a gentle summer breeze. More like a pushy autumn gale that chilled the bones, especially so when he squeezed a breast. Did he test the ripeness of a grapefruit the very same way?

Lifting up her top, he tugged it high until she was forced to bring both arms up. In his eagerness, he left the top covering her face. Aleese pulled it off. She supposed the sex could be satisfying. After all, she had trained him to give her oral—something she guessed his poor ex never got.

Keith unclasped her bra and burrowed his face in the valley between her breasts before he squeezed them tightly together so that her nipples were only inches apart. She felt like some blowup doll. He chuckled. "Almost, but not quite big enough." He let go of his treasures and tweaked the nipple of one breast between his thumb and fingernail.

Aleese winced. That was just plain mean. *What was with him? He never knew what she wanted. or maybe he didn't care.*

Keith ignored her reaction and cupping the mounds, brought his mouth down to suckle a nipple while he gripped the other breast. He always started the same way. Lips tugged enthusiastically, but instead of having an arousing effect, it made her feel used. Maybe if he said something romantic, but he didn't. She squeaked at a sudden nip and pushed his head away.

"Do you want me to..." Keith asked, tugging at her panties.

Aleese lifted her ass up, willing to try something new—anything to get a G-spot orgasm. He snatched the fabric and shoved them off, tossing them on the floor.

"Um-mm." She tried to muster up some enthusiasm, but wasn't looking forward to it.

Keith spread her legs and started to lick. She had a Golden Retriever as a child and somehow the steady up and down rhythm reminded her of the overly friendly dog. When he tightened his grip on her thighs, pinning them in place, she squirmed uncomfortably.

Mistaking her reaction as excitement, Keith dropped his towel. Shoving a pillow under her ass, he kneeled in front of her and lifted her legs up. His dick slipped in easily. Thoughts of the stranger popped back into her brain—eyes smoldering with lust.

"Ah-hh!" She sighed.

Keith gripped ankles tightly at his shoulders and thrust. This position must have aroused him. His breathing grew ragged as he picked up a rhythm.

Aleese began to feel ridiculous in this position. Her muscles tensed. Why did Keith feel this need to confine her? That vice-like grip was painfully uncomfortable. If only he'd loosen his hold or let her assume another position. She needed to rub against him. Her clit was screaming for stimulation. Aleese was tempted to get out the lube again but Keith was such a tight-ass. There's no way he'd allow it. There'd be a bruise on her thighs if he kept this up. *Stroke my clit...please!* But the Brit wouldn't. Could she do it? No-oo, he'd be angry.

Her body protested. Any second now, the pussy juices would dry up. With one last effort, Aleese fidgeted, struggling to free her ankles. An ankle slipped away from Keith's grasp and she kicked out at his shoulder.

Irritated, Keith barked, "What the hell, Aleese?" Abruptly her legs landed on the bed.

"I need to feel you," she coaxed. Tightening her pussy muscles she squeezed.

"Oh, yeah!" he groaned.

Aleese flattened her legs, lifting her hips higher to give her clit a chance to brush against him. Finally, she had just the right amount of sensation.

Keith's eyes gleamed as he heaved into her.

Aleese's hands slid down his sweat-filmed body.

Puffing with exertion, Keith muttered, "Hot little bitch, aren't you," he said, thrusting in a frenzied rhythm.

Drops of sweat tinged with a potent woodsy cologne dripped on her. She tried to block him out and imagine the sexy stranger taking her powerfully, his rod tight inside.

"Say you want it, Aleese!"

"Mm-mm," she murmured, lost in her fantasy.

"Say it!" Keith shouted, as his dick missed her G-spot.

"Touch me!" she urged, hoping he'd push his fingers into her ass. If he gave her that, she might come. But it was too late. It was over. Keith had gone limp inside her and once again, Aleese knew she was cursed.

She glanced up to see him beaming, his moustache soaking with cum. Had she really been that wet?

"Good job, Aleese. Headache gone, eh?" He pinched her nipple affectionately. "Get a shower and we'll go visit the old town. I need to pick up a few souvenirs."

Aleese took this as her cue to leave. Dragging herself up, she padded to the shower, a trickle of cum running down her inner thigh.

* * * *

Aleese didn't mind going back to the charming old colonial section of San Juan. Similar to New Orleans's French Quarter, the colorful rose, green and pale yellow buildings, had wrought iron railings around the arched windows and balconies. It would have been a fabulous stroll if it hadn't been for the company.

"I don't know how you walk in those things. You should buy yourself some practical shoes." Keith frowned at her cork platform sandals, sparkles in the leather glinting in the sunlight.

"They're no problem for me. The cobblestone is a little awkward, but the sidewalk is level. Besides, I love these sandals." Aleese thought her scarlet toenails looked particularly attractive peeking out of the straps.

Keith dropped her hand abruptly as a couple came towards them. At a narrow sidewalk, he let the other couples walk hand in hand while he stepped behind Aleese. He always did this. It would take a few minutes of walking side by side before he'd take up her hand again. Other couples strolled romantically. Not them. Some people would think he was quite the gentleman, but inwardly, Aleese thought it was because he hated the intimacy of handholding.

They'd been browsing in the tiny shops for a while now, but neither of them had bought anything. When Keith spied a store window displaying rocks and semi-precious stones, he stopped abruptly, his attention focused on some purple quartz. Aleese found the jewelry equally fascinating but she didn't think Keith would buy her any.

"You want to go in?" she asked.

"Yup. You can wait out here if you want. I saw a nice piece of quartz for my collection."

"There's some great turquoise jewelry."

"Well, come in if you wish."

Thanks, Master. She kept her sarcastic remark to herself. That's all they needed, a fight at the beginning of their vacation.

Inside the tiny shop, she eyed the turquoise pendant on the counter. When the gray-haired, bespectacled owner came over, she asked, "How much is it?"

"Thirty dollars."

"Really?"

The Chinese man nodded, his eyes inscrutable dark pools.

Having been to Mexico, Aleese knew no one just bought something at the asking price. Bargaining was standard procedure in Latin culture. Handling the turquoise, she admired the black strands in the bright stone. "Twelve dollars?"

The old man said persuasively, "You are a rich *Americana.* I am but a poor merchant."

She glanced over at Keith who was staring at her, listening to their exchange. Well, hopefully he was learning something. If he figured it out, he could bargain for the quartz. Of course, if he asked her nicely, she'd do it for him. Buying two things in one store lowered the price.

"I'm a teacher and a Canadian. We don't earn very much."

The old man's eyes narrowed. "Twenty dollars."

"Do you want the quartz, Keith?"

Keith frowned. "I'm not sure."

She smiled at the old guy. "Surely, if we buy two, you can give me a better price."

"If the gentleman buys the quartz, I am willing to give you the turquoise for eighteen."

"Fifteen and it's a deal." Aleese reached into her tote and dug out the money. The man hesitated a moment before he nodded in agreement. Wrapping her pendant in tissue, he tied a ribbon around it before he handed it to her. When she tossed it into her tote, the old man turned to Keith.

Keith asked the merchant, "How much for this piece?"

The old man displayed his yellowish teeth in a toothy smile. "Twenty dollars."

Silently, Keith gave him the money as Aleese waited.

"*Adios,*" Aleese called out happily on her way out.

Outside on the sidewalk, she reached over to grab Keith's hand, but his limply slid off hers. On the other side of the street, she recognized the café where she had seen the stranger. "That's a great café. You want to stop and have supper?"

Keith grunted. Aleese assumed that was a yes and kept on going. When they were shown a table overlooking the street, she was suddenly nervous. This was the exact table where she had sat earlier in the day. She glanced around, but was disappointed to see that the stranger wasn't there.

A waiter appeared. "*Buenos dias, señoros.*" He presented them menus. "Something to drink?"

"Beer."

"We have several, but I would recommend the Medalla."

"Right. Two beers, then." Keith opened his menu and surveyed it.

Aleese was not big on beer. It always made her feel fat and bloated, but Keith was paying and she knew they'd have only one anyway. Keith wasn't a drinker. Beer was Keith's way of melding with the natives.

"Find anything you like?" Keith asked curtly.

"A rice dish with chicken."

"Hm-mm," he said, scanning the menu. "I'm surprised you chose this place. Stuffed beef tongue and breaded calf's brains? We should have eaten at the hotel."

"It has atmosphere," Aleese said, checking out the locals walking by, "and I wanted to try something different."

Keith laughed dryly. "Different is right. Civilized people have no need to eat dog food, which I'd say," he pointed at the menu, "these items are."

"There're a lot of chicken dishes on the menu."

He didn't have a chance to comment as the waiter appeared with their beer.

"Could you recommend a chicken dish for my friend?" Aleese asked.

"*Asopao* or the *arroz con pollo*. Are you very hungry, *señor*?"

"Reasonably so."

"Then perhaps the *arroz con pollo*. It is the specialty of the house."

"We'll both have it, right?"

Aleese nodded. At least they were in agreement with this. She'd been afraid he'd drag her out of the café and insist on roast beef at the hotel.

As they waited for their order, Keith tapped his fingers impatiently. His jaw clenched as he sat staring out at the passing crowd.

This was Aleese's first vacation since she'd started teaching two years ago. To go on spring break vacation to a place with a decent beach meant booking six months in advance. She didn't have any close female friends and since Keith had been eager to explore San Juan, she'd booked it with him, splitting the cost. But glancing at Keith's sullen composure, she wished she'd gone by herself. It was altogether too stressful to be with him. He liked to sulk until she dug the truth out of him. Most of the time, she had to apologize to smooth his ruffled feathers. Obviously from the look on his face, he was punishing her for some slight. What was it this time?

Aleese's thoughts drifted to the stranger. Sex had been bearable because of her fantasy man. Right now with Keith giving her the silent treatment, she immersed herself in the memory of the man she'd only fleetingly seen. What had he been thinking when their eyes met?

From inside the restaurant, the band played a sultry salsa. The seductive music made her think of his forearms, exposed by the white shirt. He'd been slim and strong. Keith wasn't short, but when she had her high heels on, he was almost eye level. There was something very attractive about a tall muscular man, she mused, visualizing the dark-haired stranger.

When the chicken with yellow rice arrived, she was sure Keith would lighten up. Something to do with his blood sugar level. He wasn't a diabetic, but had problems if he didn't eat on schedule. When he explained this to her, he'd go on about his need to eat immediately or he'd be ill. After the fifth glycolic sequel, she tuned him out.

Sure enough, Keith took the dinner as his cue to focus on the meal. He didn't seem to mind not talking while eating. He'd told her it had to do with boarding school back in England. If a boy wanted seconds, he'd have to eat fast or be left with nothing.

Aleese downed some beer and found it agreeable, even though she would have preferred wine. Her former boyfriend had been a maître d' with a penchant for aged burgundies. He'd hooked her on reds. Lately, she'd tried almost every kind of Australian Shiraz available. With this chicken she would have enjoyed a deeply flavorful berried wine, but it was not to be. Keith had decided she should drink the local beer. It wasn't a pleasant meal. In between mouthfuls, he stared at her, eyes accusingly shooting daggers.

Otherwise, the dinner was delightful. In fact, as the waiter removed their plates, Aleese started thinking about a scrumptious dessert—chocolate mousse would finish the dinner perfectly. "Excuse me," she called out to the waiter rounding their table, "would it be possible to get a dessert menu?"

"*Si, señorita,*" he said, "I will be right back."

She glanced over at Keith, who was examining his fingernail. "Wasn't that old man funny?"

"What?"

"The old man in the shop. I think he gave me a good price. What about your quartz?"

"It was reasonable, Aleese. In fact, everything was reasonable, Aleese—except you!"

"What do you mean?"

Keith glared. "You were inexcusably rude. I have never been so embarrassed in my life!"

Surely he wasn't referring to Aleese negotiating for the jewelry. She'd been so proud of herself for pulling off that deal. "You mean because I bargained for the turquoise?" Aleese asked hesitantly, completely thrown off by his accusation.

The waiter returned with a dessert menu and Aleese opened it up.

"What do you think, Aleese?" He motioned for the waiter to return. "Check."

Aleese stiffened. *It was customary to bargain, wasn't it? What did he mean?*

The server took Keith's credit card and trotted off.

"But…"

"It was the most humiliating experience. Can't you see we are in a third world country, Aleese? I'd bet the Chinese fellow doesn't even have a pension plan." He signed the bill and pocketed his card.

A knot twisted in the pit of her stomach. Maybe, Keith was right. Bargaining shouldn't have been her priority. She should have paid the old man what he had asked. Her shoulders slumped in her misery. But a glimpse of a tall dark-haired man entering the restaurant pushed her guilt to a back-burner. With a family leaving another table, her view was blocked. She peered around Keith but didn't see where he had gone.

Keith stood up. "I paid. Come on."

"I want to stay and have dessert."

"I don't want to stay."

Something welled up inside of Aleese—pent up anger and frustration topped with an abundance of hurt. "Go, then!"

Between closed teeth, Keith hissed, "Aleese!"

He looked as if he would have liked to have dragged her out by the hair, but his rigid private school training won out and all he could do was stand there and glare.

Aleese gazed at him defiantly and said, "I'm staying."

Keith's eyes narrowed, but he didn't argue. His jaw clenched, he spun around on his heel and strode out the café without another word.

Aleese half expected him to come back and apologize. Her eyes watered. She hadn't done anything wrong—he wouldn't make her cry. And then she panicked. The hotel—could she find it? Inhaling deeply, Aleese calmed down, recalling the route back. But walking alone at night—not safe. Was there enough money for a taxi? Aleese frowned. In her purse, she spotted a twenty dollar bill peeking out from the side compartment. She sighed in relief.

"Would you like a moment to decide on a dessert, *señorita*?" the waiter asked from behind her shoulder, "...or?"

Aleese started. She glanced down at the menu in confusion.

The waiter pointed. Her eyes followed his finger to the dessert selections. Methodically she read, hardly understanding what was before her. A tear drop welled up and slid down her cheek. She was beginning to regret her impulsiveness.

"*Polvo de amor*," a husky voice said softly from over her shoulder.

Aleese glanced up and met the smoldering dark eyes of the stranger. Heart racing, she stared speechlessly.

His lips twitched. "It's not as good as chocolate, but I'm sure you'll enjoy it."

"Chocolate?" Aleese's forehead furrowed. "How did you..."

"Know?" Wavy dark hair blew onto his forehead. He gave her an engaging smile. "I was moved by the way you ate that croissant this morning. You enjoyed it so much." He motioned to the chair next to her. "May I join you?"

Aleese nodded, speechless—her brain waves spinning.

The stranger sat down beside her. Leaning back, he stretched out his long, jean-clad legs, and tilting his head gazed over. He said his name quickly, the word flowing musically, "Arman."

Arman? Aleese was confused, lost in the mysterious waters of his whisky eyes, but when he raised an eyebrow, she pulled herself together enough to return, "Aleese."

He reached over, his hand outstretched and she gave him hers, but instead of shaking it, he met her eyes a second before he slowly brought it up to his lips and kissed her wrist. Shivers raced down Aleese's body. She waited, but he didn't release her hand. He studied her. Placing his other hand on top of hers, he let it rest there lightly while he spoke. "I'm glad I caught up with you again."

His deeply masculine voice activated tingles in her pussy. "We didn't really meet," she murmured.

Arman released her hands. "No. You left too soon."

"*Señorita, señor*," the waiter said sidling up to them. "Sorry to interrupt. Have you decided?"

"We'll both have the *polvo de amor*," Arman said. "Is that alright, Aleese?"

The waiter took up the beer glasses and waited.

Aleese nodded uncertainly. She watched silently as the waiter made his way to the rear of the restaurant. Turning to Arman, she asked curiously, "What does that mean—*polvo de amor?*"

"Love powder." Arman laughed.

Aleese's eyes widened.

"Coconut baked in the oven. It's an island favorite."

"Oh."

"Next time, I'll get you something with chocolate."

"You will?"

His dark eyes shimmered golden. "Yeah."

The waiter suddenly appeared, and deposited their dessert with a flourish.

"Thank you," Aleese said distractedly.

"Try it," Arman said, watching her.

Dipping her spoon in, Aleese cautiously took a mouthful.

The dessert was crispy yet soft—an interesting combination that stimulated her taste buds. "It's good."

"Good," he repeated, smiling. "I can see we must find a chocolate dessert or your faith in Puerto Rico will be lost."

"No-oo, I really do like it."

"Don't worry. I understand. I know how chocolate makes you feel."

"You do?"

"I have a love of chocolate that transcends rational thought."

Aleese relaxed. "I've never met a man that loves chocolate. What I mean is, men say they like chocolate, but none of them have chocolate cravings." She thought of Keith and how he'd laughed when she'd finished the box of Lindt he'd given her for Valentine's Day, all in an afternoon. It had been a condescending type of laugh, as if she were somewhat flawed for enjoying it so much.

"We could have a chocolate feast."

Aleese paused in the middle of a mouthful and fantasized Arman covered in chocolate. She would be licking up the dark creamy chocolate, starting at those full sensuous lips. Her mouth would suck up a truffle strategically placed at his nipple and then journey south.

Tilting his head, Arman stared at her, his mouth curled slightly up at the corners. "What did you imagine?"

Aleese blushed and hurriedly scooped up some more coconut dessert.

"Tell me. Did you like what you saw?" Arman pressed.

"Um-mm."

"Will you let me in on it?"

"Maybe."

Arman's eyebrows raised questioningly. He sat back and gazed at her thoughtfully.

"I was thinking about you," Aleese admitted hesitantly.

"And I you. All day." He forked up a chunk of dessert.

"Intermittently, of course. What were you thinking?

"I wondered if you'd come back."

"I was passing by tonight when I saw you."

"Deliberately?"

"I live near here." Shoving his bowl away, Arman asked, "Are you finished?"

Aleese nodded.

"Good. Do you feel like walking?"

"Sure. Where to?"

"I'm tempted to show you my condo—we could sit outside and have some wine."

"But?"

"But it's a little crowded today."

"Why?"

"My roommates just came back."

"From where?"

"New York."

"Lucky them. Vacation?"

"They're flight attendants with American Airlines—we all are."

"Oh-hh!" Aleese sighed. A guy in a uniform—why did that turn her on so much? She looked at him suspiciously. He must know how hot he was and how women liked uniforms.

"Where are you staying?" Arman asked.

Why did life seem so much like a classroom—comments and questions just like show and tell. If she confessed to being on vacation with Keith, Arman might leave and that would be the end of the beginning. Aleese bit her lip. But if she did tell him, she wouldn't have to worry about being a slut and succumbing to her urges.

"Aleese?"

She gathered her thoughts. "The Del Mar Hotel."

Arman looked as if he were about to comment on that when the waiter appeared with the check. Before Aleese could reach for her tote, he paid. "It's on me," Arman said, standing up. "Come, I'll show you my favorite bar."

He took her hand and they wove their way around the tables to the door. His hand was warm and his touch was electric. She glanced up at his rugged features—a strong chin, full lips and a long slightly hooked nose combined asymmetrically, yet every imperfection oozed sexuality in a way that pricked her nerve endings.

The night air was balmy and warm—sea salt in the breeze. Bordering the sidewalk, palm fronds swayed softly. Occasionally, a group passed by and Arman would wrap his arm around her and pull her close to allow them to pass.

"Is it far?" Aleese asked, glancing into Arman's changeable eyes.

"A block or two."

Aleese gazed down at her platform shoes. Walkable, she thought.

"You look good with high heels."

She smiled. "I like wearing them. I know they're not practical."

"Practical is boring."

She shot him a look.

"Useful, practical and logical—all boring. Necessary at times, but ultimately hum-drum."

"Oh." Aleese didn't know what to say to that. Keith was always telling her to be more practical.

"You are small." Arman studied her. "A pixie."

Was he joking? "You mean like a fairy?"

"No, you're pixie material."

"Pixies are," Aleese mulled this over, "naughty?"

"And mischievous."

"Hm-mm. Haven't been much of that lately."

"No?" Arman smiled slowly, pushing his dark waves away from his eyes. "Change is a positive thing." He glanced at a building set back from the street. "That's it."

Down a narrow road, there was an open-air bar with a palapa roof. As they approached, Aleese could hear the rush of the ocean. The floor was raised and the seats surrounding the oval wooden bar were wide swing chairs. Lanterns lit the area, casting an inviting yellow glow.

"*Hola,*" the bartender called out. "How's it going, man?"

"Great. Hey, Emilio, I'd like you to meet my friend, Aleese."

"Welcome, *señorita.*" Flashing pearly whites, he grinned widely. His café au lait coloring spoke of his mixed heritage. "Watch him. He's fast." he warned. "You won't know what hit you."

"Don't listen to Emilio. He's *loco*—the girls run when they see him coming."

On the other side of the bar, a couple of men snickered at that remark. Aleese looked over at a blond man and his slender companion, dashing in their blue uniforms. Pilots or maybe…

"Flight attendants," Arman whispered in her ear as the blond nodded in his direction. "Hey, Jack. How's it goin'?"

"Can't be better. First day of layover," the blond drawled. "How are you, Arman?"

"I'm good."

The dark-haired man next to Jack waved.

"Hey! Talk to you guys later, 'kay?" Arman's eyes shot to an empty swing chair. "Let's sit in that one."

Aleese placed a hand on the wide rattan chair. Suspended by thick ropes from the rafters, it swayed with the sea breeze. "Will it hold us?"

His heavy-lidded eyes gleamed in the dim light. "It's strong. We'll fit nicely." He held the chair steady for her to climb into.

On tip toes, she grasped the rope before she thrust herself into the basket. Backed against the cushion, her legs dangled over the edge.

"I'll take your shoes off," Arman said, without waiting for her reply. Slipping them off, he set them on the wooden planked flooring. His eyes slowly swept down the length of her body. "Beautiful legs, perfect for high heels."

Aleese smiled shyly, pleased by his compliment.

"You want your usual," Emilio called out, "and perhaps a piña colada for the lovely lady?"

"Aleese?"

"That sounds nice." In fact everything was nice—the moon peeking from behind the clouds, the sea-scented breeze and the white caps glistening in the dark Caribbean waters visible from her vantage point in the swing. It was magical.

"Could you hold these?" Arman asked, handing her two drinks as he slid in beside her. "Emilio knows how to make an exceptional piña colada."

The creamy-white drink was in a plastic glass, but every care had been taken to make the drink a decorative masterpiece—a scarlet hibiscus flower adorning the edge along with a slice of pineapple.

"Relax, Aleese. Put your feet on my lap."

An offer she couldn't refuse. Leaning back against the cushion, her feet on his jean clad thigh, Aleese sipped her drink. "Arman is an unusual name."

"French."

"Oh, I thought you might be Puerto Rican."

"My mother is. Taught me Spanish—a requirement for the job." Arman's lips curled up at the ends. "Your name suits you. *Für Elise*. A haunting piece. Beethoven must have had you in mind."

Aleese felt her cheeks grow hot. "Not quite. My father wanted me to have a traditional German name and he would have won, but for once, my mom stuck to her guns. It's a different spelling, too. My mom wanted me to be an original."

Arman tipped back his beer before he murmured, "And you are."

"What makes you say that?"

"Everything about you."

"Now you're doing exactly what Emilio said."

"Which is?"

"Saying things to flatter me."

Reaching out to the bar, Arman set his bottle down. "You are far too wise to fall for that from a mere mortal."

"Because I'm a pixie, right?"

Arman's lips turned up slightly at the corners. "You're a pixie goddess—a tricky beauty with secrets."

How did he know? Had he seen Keith leave? Aleese frowned.

Arman picked up her foot and examined her toenail artistry. "A dainty, pretty foot." Holding it with one hand, he stroked it with the other. "Tell me about you. Why did you come to San Juan?"

His question was easier than she'd anticipated. "It's school break and I'm a teacher. I thought San Juan sounded lovely from the brochure and," her eyes lit on the ocean, "it is."

"The island has more than white beaches and casinos."

Aleese nodded. "History."

"Would you like to see the fort with me?"

"You have time?"

"I have a few days before I head back."

That wasn't a long time. Aleese didn't know why, but that made her suddenly sad. After all, they had just met.

Leaning back in the chair, she closed her eyes. At first, light strokes caressed her foot in the most pleasing manner. And then his thumbs took up the job, solidly pushing against her instep in a circular motion, releasing all her stress and at the same time, awakening her senses. When he suddenly brought a foot up to his mouth, she giggled. What was he doing? The pressure of his lips sucking her toe jolted her like low voltage electricity. Aleese squirmed unprepared for the pleasure of his assault. A soft moan escaped.

He withdrew his lips only to tighten them on another toe. She could hardly hold on to her drink the tingling between her thighs was all she could think about. "Arman," she whispered.

Still sucking her toe, he eyed her a moment before he stopped and released her foot. "You're very tasty."

She hardly knew what to say. No one had ever done anything like that to her. Massaged her feet, yes—a New Year's party. The guy had been nice, but there was zero attraction there or she might have clued in that he was hitting on her. But in this case, the man was hot and she was getting tingles just sitting here.

"We'll go to the beach tomorrow for a while and later go to the fort?"

Later. After what? There was a gap there. "Mm-mm."

He grinned. "I take that as a yes?"

What was she thinking? She couldn't. There was Keith. But if she didn't tell him… "I could meet you at the beach."

"That would work."

"Where?" Aleese asked.

"The beach at your hotel? I'll bring a blanket, towels and drinks. You bring…"

"Sunscreen?"

"You." Arman sat back and closed his eyes a second before he opened them. Speaking softly, he said, "I'm seeing a sexy woman in a bikini."

"Bikini?"

"You have one, don't you?"

"Of course," she said, thinking she'd better go shopping for a matching cover-up tomorrow. She had to look hotter than hot.

"Then I'll look forward to it. All night, I'll dream of us on that perfect stretch of sand."

"Is it—perfect? I haven't been to the beach."

"No? When did you arrive?"

"Yesterday. In the afternoon." Keith had decided they should shower and have sex. She'd missed the sunset, too.

"But you've seen it?"

"From my balcony. The water is brilliantly blue and the beach is wide."

"The island has great beaches. What else do you like?"

"I like…" she hesitated, not knowing what he wanted to hear—something concrete or something more elusive.

"I don't mean sports or hobbies."

"Freedom."

"Interesting. You're not free?"

"I'm free and I'm single. And you?" She waited anxiously, sure that his answer would disappoint her. Someone that delicious must be taken.

"I was captured, but I'm free now."

Aleese took another sip of her drink and thought about his choice of words. "Captured. That's a funny word to describe a relationship. You were married?"

"I was in love. We lived together for a year."

"And it made you feel bad?"

"Only later. At first it was everything I ever wanted." Arman's whiskey eyes glimmered in the dim light. "And you, goddess? Have you felt that all consuming feeling that mortals call love?"

"I'm not sure." This brought thoughts of Keith back to mind. Was he in the room now, waiting for her? He'd be angry. "I need to go, Arman."

Arman raised an eyebrow. "You're not a night person?"

"Sometimes. I can be, but I need to do some things tomorrow morning and I'm afraid I'm a bit jet-lagged."

"A goddess needs her sleep, I suppose." He slipped off the seat, took her glass and helped her down. Taking out his wallet, he threw some bills on the counter.

Aleese heard light tinkling laughter. In the glow of the lantern, a striking brunette with long wavy hair, her bangs side-swept over one eye, stood between the two flight attendants.

Arman's eyes flicked to the woman. "Come, let me introduce

you," he said, his husky voice to her ear. Taking her hand he brought her over to the group on the far side of the round bar. The woman in a clingy white dress, her chest thrust out, was the focus of all the males at the bar. Emilio had let his beer glasses soak in the sink to lean in to hear her throaty comment. She teased him with her finger bringing it to his lips. Aleese felt vaguely envious.

Whatever the siren was about to say, she forgot as she swung around, her large brown eyes taking them in. "Arman! They didn't tell me you were here. Now I know why." she said, her voice smooth as silk, studying Aleese. "Who is your lovely *amiga*?"

Aleese felt suddenly embarrassed at the way this woman examined her so intently, but she extended her hand politely. "Aleese."

"*Bellesica*." The woman ignored her hand and pulled her close, planting a kiss on each cheek. "My name is Francisca, but they call me Cisca." She turned to Arman. "Where did you find this flower?"

"You must get out more, Cisca."

"Always the man of mystery. Watch out for him, Aleese. He'll charm you."

Jack chuckled. "Emilio already warned her."

"But they never listen, do they?" she said speaking to the men before she turned to Aleese again. "I'm Arman's roommate."

The trim dark-haired man beside Jack spoke up, "And I'm his roommate, Jamy."

"Hi," Aleese said.

"Hey, nice to meet you. Why don't we go, Jack? Arman can take care of the ladies."

Jack smirked. "Maybe Cisca would rather come with us."

"All right," Cisca purred, "why don't I? Arman already has his *pescado*."

Jack slid off his swing chair and took her elbow. "Coming, Jamy?"

Jamy followed the pair reluctantly.

When they disappeared around the corner, Aleese had to ask, "What was that all about?"

"What?"

"I sensed Jack liked Cisca, but what's with Jamy?"

"Jealous."

"Well, she is attractive and Jack is the one she likes…"

"Not that simple, Aleese. Jack is bi. He's been after Cisca for weeks. This is the first time she's noticed him."

"And Jamy? He likes her, too?"

"Come," Arman said, taking her hand. Once out of the bar, he explained with a grin, "Jamy's in love with Jack."

"Oh-hh!"

They started walking on the sidewalk before, he continued, "Cisca likes the drama."

"Are Jack and Jamy together?"

"No. Jack is a player."

"And Cisca?"

Arman laughed. "She's a law unto herself." He stopped to stare at the high-rise hotel ahead. "You like it?"

"The Hotel Del Mar?"

"Yeah."

"I'm on the seventh floor and the view is breathtaking." It would have been romantic with the right person to share it with…

"I'd like to see it."

Wouldn't she just love to be standing on the balcony, his arm around her, watching the waves roll in, but there was Keith. "Rain check?"

"I like the rain."

"Me too. It's romantic…" she mused, "walks in the rain."

"And thunderstorms. Like them?"

"The clouds rolling in, the rumble and then the flash. Yes, very much."

They neared the revolving door of the white building. Arman stepped back to let her go in. She brought out her hand to stop him from following. "I'll see you tomorrow, okay?"

Arman gazed at her curiously before he said, "I'll meet you out on the beach at one. Bring a change of clothes and we'll see the fort afterwards."

"One question. Something puzzled me."

"Yes?"

"Why did Cisca call me a *pescado*? What does that mean?"

His dark eyes glowed in the lamp light. "A *pescado* is a hooked fish." He ran a finger down her cheek. "But maybe I'm the one that's hooked and you're a mermaid goddess."

* * * *

Aleese didn't feel like much of a goddess of any kind as she walked into the lobby. She was in a fix and she knew it.

Off to the right of the lobby, she noticed the casino. She hadn't been in there yet. The concept of playing blackjack with wealthy jet-setters perked her fancy. It wouldn't hurt to appease her curiosity and at the same time avoid the inevitable confrontation with Keith.

The Del Mar casino was not in the least like casinos in Vegas. It was quiet. The slot machines were in another room outside the casino. Inside, the croupiers spoke in hushed whispers and the plush red carpet dulled the gamblers' voices. Each blackjack table was marked with a minimum bet ranging from ten dollars to five hundred dollars. Craps and poker tables were situated in the corner. Waiters strolled around serving the players.

Aleese was invited to sit at a table but she shook her head and explained she was only watching. She wished she had brought some money with her because in her unconscious mind she knew she had a gambling itch that ached to be scratched, but she also had a cautious side that combated that wild side.

In the course of a half hour, she wandered from table to table observing the game and the people playing. Many were obviously wealthy, unless of course the diamonds were fake, but to her untrained eye, they had that special sparkle that was undeniably real. She was just about to give in to temptation and sit at a table when she spotted a man in a charcoal suit with his back to her. He was playing blackjack at the hundred dollar minimum bet table. It was Keith.

There was no point in staying now. Exiting the casino, she rushed to the elevator. Luckily, he hadn't seen her. It wasn't something she had expected. Keith was logical and to her mind, unexciting—not exactly gambler material. But as an engineer, he knew his math. He could easily count cards. She frowned. No one would have thought she were the type either, but if Aleese had been prepared, she would have chanced playing just to have had the opportunity to play in a proper casino, the European type featured in Bond movies.

But she had more to lose by staying. There'd be no conflict if she were in bed asleep. Satisfied with her problem-solving, she hustled into the elevator.

Once in the room, she hurried to brush her teeth and remove her makeup. The last thing she wanted was sex with Keith, so she quickly donned a pair of boxers and a top. Settling herself in bed, her mind wandered to Arman and how delicious he'd looked in his white shirt and jeans.

Unconsciously, her fingers slid under her top and smoothed over her breast, circling and kneading her nipple. She pulled on her already swelling nub and imagined Arman's hand cupping her breast and his lips sucking her nipple to hardness. She felt an ache between her thighs. Bringing her other hand down into her boxers, she stroked the velvety folds that covered her clit.

Spreading her legs slightly allowed her fingers easier access. Her clit was moist. Sliding her finger further down between the lips of her pussy, she stuck a finger inside before bringing her exploration back to her clit. Arman's rugged features and his enigmatic whiskey eyes flashed in her mind. Fingers tightened around her nipple. His tongue would lick the valley between her breasts. She let her fingernails lightly graze her skin, as they trailed from her breast to belly button where her hand rested on her silken skin.

Would he like the way she tasted? Did he really mean that? Would he want to bring his lips to her clit and tease her with his tongue, savoring her scent and her juices? Her forefinger stayed on the bud of her clit and she stroked it until her body writhed lost in the rhythm. Aleese floated in the sensation. Her breathing becoming ragged, she almost didn't hear the click of the door. But there was no mistaking Keith's voice.

"Aleese?" he called out. "Are you there? Wake up. You'd never guess—I won."

She curled up in a fetal position, her eyes shut, Aleese pretended to breathe deeply as if she were asleep.

He shuffled around before he approached the bed and sat down. She heard his shoes hit the floor with a bang. It was getting harder to pretend to be asleep with all the noise he was making. When a belt-buckle clanged on the tiles, Aleese figured the rest of his clothes had joined the shoes.

Lifting the covers, Keith shoved himself close. "Celebration time, Aleese. To the victor go the spoils." He chuckled. "In this case, guess who gets spoiled?" He touched her ass. "What's this? Clothes?" He tugged at her boxers pushing them down over the curve of her butt. "Lift up."

When she didn't respond, he edged right up to her. She could feel his hard cock poking into the fabric. "Come on, Aleese. I know you're awake." He groped her breast, but she rolled away from him onto her stomach.

Not to be ignored, Keith tugged once again on her boxers. "You like it this way…"

"No," she murmured.

"Come on. You know you like it."

He didn't get any further as fury built up inside her. Forming a fist, Aleese backhanded Keith across the face.

It must have hurt. The squawk sounded a bit like her cat when she accidentally stepped on his tail. "Aleese! What the hell?"

"I'm sleeping."

She heard the bed clunk as Keith got out and this time she didn't pretend. Feeling tremendously exhausted, she sighed and drifted into a deep sleep.

2

Sparkling turquoise water lapped onto a wide expanse of sandy shore. With just a smattering of sun worshippers dotting the area, it wasn't hard for Aleese to find Arman.

Standing at the edge of the beach, his legs hip-width apart, he stood looking into the distance. She let her eyes travel down the length of his lanky frame. His powerful shoulders and strong back narrowed to a slim waist. As she continued her journey south, his bathing suit covered a firm curved ass and where it stopped, a pair of muscular legs.

With the afternoon sun behind him, she visualized his tanned body nude. She would be stroking him from top to bottom, paying special attention to his firm erection. It would be kissable, she was certain of that. Aleese wanted to resist these thoughts, but her pussy wouldn't let her. It tingled and contracted as if to receive the stiff cock he'd have for her.

Suddenly, he swung around, as if sensing her approach. "Aleese." Taking her hands in his, he stepped back to take a look at her. "Gorgeous woman. No, I'm wrong—you're a goddess come to visit."

Aleese felt herself flush at his words. No one had ever complimented her like that.

"I wasn't sure if you'd eaten." He gestured to a blanket on the beach. "I brought some pâté and a bottle of Shiraz."

"Perfect." Aleese unwrapped her gold lamé cover-up, threw it on the blanket and sat down beside Arman. "How did you know I liked Shiraz?"

"What goddess wouldn't?" He handed her a wine glass and a serviette. "Hungry?"

"Mm-mm." She hadn't eaten breakfast or lunch.

Arman took out crackers, a jar of pâté and a knife. "How was your morning?"

"Busy. I did some shopping." Aleese had woken early, packed her tote and left before Keith had even stirred. It had taken her forever to find a boutique that carried a matching cover-up for her gold metallic bikini, but she had wanted to be irresistible for Arman and by the look in his eyes, she had succeeded.

"And what does a goddess shop for?"

Aleese smirked. "Anything she wants."

"Then I hope I'm on your list."

She sipped her wine, giving Arman a sultry glance over the rim of her glass. "You want to be?"

"A goddess needs to be worshipped…" Arman offered her a cracker coated with pâté. "Would you like that?"

Aleese stared heavenward, chewing contemplatively before she gazed back at him in amusement. "How?"

A hint of a smile formed on his lips as he replied, "Spontaneously."

Aleese imagined them passionately wrestling on the blanket. Shocked, people would get up and leave, but some would be so fascinated they'd stay and watch.

"I'd love to read your mind."

"No one has ever worshipped me before."

"Then it's time."

"I suppose. But soon you'll be flying back to New York?"

"Toronto."

"Really? How strange. That's where I live. Well, not quite there—on the outskirts. But I thought…"

"I've been flying New York to San Juan, but I needed a change and my family lives there." He poured some more wine into his glass.

Her heart had been pounding ever since he said he would be in Toronto. "So you'll be flying Toronto to San Juan?"

"For a while. I've been offered a ground job."

"Not as exciting, I guess," Aleese said quietly, thinking he wouldn't want a job like that.

Arman smiled slowly. "It could be."

"What about flying? Won't you miss it?"

"I've had seven years of it."

"The seven year itch."

He laughed. "That's usually about relationships." Arman's eyes became intense. "You had one of those?"

"It's hard for me to reach the seven month itch."

"Ah-hh. A free-spirited goddess?"

Aleese spread a cracker with pâté and considered his question. "Circumstances got in the way and the men were totally wrong for me."

"Love is elusive."

"It's not just a chemical thing. There has to be more." Both she and Keith had similar values and he was solid and dependable. She munched the cracker reflectively. Keith wanted marriage and he'd told her she was the right woman for him. His intentions were honorable, although a bit traditional.

"It can't exist without that magical feeling that moves the spirit."

"Says a man that's been captured."

"Only with her. She wanted my body, my mind and my spirit."

Something was nagging her in the back of her mind. "There's just so much you can do for another person before you lose yourself."

Arman took her hand and gently stroked it. "You know what I'm saying, don't you?"

"I think so." Aleese liked the way he touched her. It was difficult to keep her mind on their conversation with his hand on hers. What would it be like to be touched all over?

"Why don't you lie down? I'll put sunscreen on your back."

"Okay." Aleese stretched out on the blanket.

He handed her a wine glass and she sipped it before she said, "Values and work ethics have to be similar for a couple to make it."

Warming the lotion in his hands, Arman spread it gently on Aleese. Starting at her shoulders he smoothed it down her back to her bikini bottom. "Work is necessary. Basic values are important. But, in my experience, ideas can change."

"I'm not sure about marriage." Aleese couldn't quite picture herself in an apron cooking roast beef for Keith. "I don't even know if I want to live with anyone. Seems to me, it just causes problems. I think I'd rather date."

Arman stroked her thighs and Aleese forgot everything else she wanted to say.

"When two people are right, they'll know," he said in his husky voice.

"Mm-mm." Aleese didn't know what she was agreeing to—the

sensation in her pussy was driving her wild. If he stroked her inner thighs, she'd start moaning and the beach police would issue a warrant for her arrest—lewd behavior in a public place.

Arman dropped the sunscreen in the side pocket of his cooler. He brought himself down beside her. Refilling their glasses he clicked his glass to hers, and said, "*Salud.*"

With his face so close to hers, Aleese was tongue-tied.

"Your eyes…a beautiful Caribbean blue."

Such full sensuous lips. What would it be like to kiss them?

"Aleese…"

Her heart skipped a beat when his mouth pressed down on hers. A soft tender kiss that lingered until her lips parted for his tongue to enter. He licked the sensitive area inside her lips. She pushed her tongue eagerly back, until she realized they were on a beach. People were watching them. Withdrawing, Aleese leaned back.

"What's wrong?"

"I felt strange."

"Because?"

Aleese flicked her eyes at a couple near them. "They made me feel uncomfortable."

"Life is too short to worry about trivial things. Never mind them. They're jealous."

Aleese smiled. "Of?"

"Our chemistry." He inclined his head. "Look at them, Aleese."

Her eyes landed on the middle-aged couple watching them—the woman, attractive except for her pinched lips and narrowed eyes. The man's hanging jowls reminded her of a bull dog.

"If they ever had any passion, it's long gone." Arman regarded her. "I like the taste of your lips—sweet like chocolate."

"Thank you." His lips were irresistible. And the rest of him needed to be sampled as soon as possible. But what about Keith? He'd expect her tonight—back in his bed.

"You look worried."

"I was thinking about the fort. Does it take long to get there?"

Arman dug out his cell phone from the pocket of his bathing suit and glanced at the digital clock. "Why don't we leave soon? That should give us enough time to shower and change. The fort closes at five."

"Shower?"

"You'll feel better."

"Where?" If Aleese went back to the hotel room, Keith might be there and that would be trouble.

"At my condo, remember? It will save us time. You did bring some clothes to change into?"

"Mm-mm. And your roommates?"

"We won't be there long." He gave her a heavy-lidded gaze. "You'll love the fort."

"It's a Spanish fort, isn't it?"

"I'll tell you all about it, when we get there. Ready to leave?"

"Sure." Aleese passed him her wine glass.

After packing it all up, Arman took her hand and they left the beach, heading for the street. Aleese had her beach clothes on, but when she saw everyone in street clothes she wondered if she shouldn't have slipped on her top and skirt.

"Arman, I think I need to cover up," she said hesitantly.

"Not a problem." They had come to a stop at a motor scooter. "Here we are." At the back, he had a carrier where he stuck the cooler and blanket. Tugging out two t-shirts from a back pack, he handed one to Aleese. "Wear this one," he said, pulling the other over his head. "You don't want to grease up your clothes."

As she tugged it on she caught a scent of citron mixed with male—a delicious heady scent that made her imagine his naked body beneath her. The green t-shirt was large and covered her like a mini-dress.

"You look cute, goddess."

Her eyes swept down to her bare thighs. "Thanks. I must look bizarre. And Arman, I have to warn you. I've never been on a motor scooter."

"First time is always a thrill." He tossed her tote bag in the carrier.

"And the second?"

Arman smiled. "Every ride can be exciting."

Somehow Aleese knew he was not referring to the ride or was it another type of ride he was thinking about? Climbing on behind him, she hugged his waist and visualized herself on top of him in cowboy position. He'd like that—rubbing her clit against him as she brought her breasts to his mouth. Aleese imagined herself rocking his stiff tool until they both came together in an explosive orgasm.

Arman revved the engine and pulled out into the street. With her cheek brushing his back, the wind in her face, and the scent and warmth of his body she felt exhilarated. The scooter swerved in and out of heavy city traffic and Aleese clung to him, her face flushed with excitement.

The ride was almost too brief. At the top of the hill, Arman parked and helped her off. He grabbed the backpack and cooler and she followed him to a white stucco house with a red tile roof. A black wrought-iron fence bordered the property. Reaching in, Arman undid the latch of the gate and motioned for Aleese to go through.

He grinned. "Do you think there's a chance we might be alone?" Not waiting for her response, he opened the wide oak door for her to enter the hallway. A wood framed still-life in deep earth tones hung on the terra cotta walls.

"Lovely," Aleese exclaimed.

"The paintings are Cisca's. She dabbles."

"I heard that!" a lilting voice called out. Cisca in a long white robe, danced down the hall towards them. "I dabble, but he paints." She swung Aleese around and pointed at a large canvas in a lounge. "See the nude? See how she bows her head. She's depressed that he's left her." A brunette with wavy brown hair sitting on a couch with her back to the viewer watched a man outside her window. "Recognize the model?"

Aleese stared at the voluptuous woman in the painting and then brought her eyes back to Cisca. "Is it you?" She glanced at Arman. "And you're the artist?"

"I'm afraid so."

"Cisca you look lovely and Arman, you are very talented."

Arman ran his hand down her cheek. "Thanks, babe. You're both beautiful, but you," he whispered in her ear, "are a goddess."

Cisca snorted. "I heard that. That's not what you used to think. I can remember when…"

"That's the past. I'm sure Aleese is not interested."

"I'm cooking tonight. You two staying for dinner?"

"No. Aleese needs to take a shower and then we're leaving. Could you show her where it is?"

Cisca smiled. "Certainly. Come, Aleese," she said, taking her arm and linking it with hers.

At the end of the hallway, Cisca steered Aleese to the right and opened the door for her. "You'll find everything you need inside. I'll be right next door," she called back over her shoulder. "By the way, the door doesn't lock but you'll be fine," Cisca added with a smile.

The room was tiled in white—floor and walls. A bubbly transparent curtain covered the entrance to a large walk-in shower. Wasting no time, Aleese slipped off her clothes and stepped in. Adjusting the jets to a warm spray, she rinsed off. On a shelf, Aleese located a shampoo. It was regular shampoo providing no clue as to whether its owner was feminine or masculine. With a few drops in her wet hair she lathered, wondering all the while where Arman was. Could there be another shower in the house or was he waiting for her to finish?

Steamy air had escaped the shower curtain. With the room a hazy mist, she didn't notice the figure coming towards her, but there was no mistaking the voice. "Brought you some shower gel."

"Thanks," Aleese said, reaching out of the stall.

It was then that she noticed Cisca. Nude and beautiful—apple-shaped breasts tipped with prominent brown nipples partially covered by long wavy hair. Glancing down, Aleese was surprised. Not a single pubic hair. She must have been staring because Cisca laughed. "I see you believe in a more natural look. Pretty, though. It must be because your blonde hair is so fine." She put her finger on Aleese's belly and trailed down. "You shave, but I can hardly detect a hair. You don't get much growth?"

"No," Aleese said, slightly uncomfortable. "Did you want something?"

"Relax, *cariño*." She dabbed a drop of gel in her hand and applied it to Aleese's back. "Hope you like jasmine."

The fragrance of sweet flowers filled the air.

"Thank you, but I don't need any help."

"This will feel good." Cisca stroked Aleese's shoulders and back and brought her hands down to the curve of Aleese's ass. "Wow, you must work out. You have hardly any fat and good muscle tone." She dropped another dab on her hand. "I had another reason to come in. I hope you don't mind, but I had to have a quick shower." She glanced down. "I'm so sticky." With her hand she spread the gel on her belly. "Jack got so wild he sprayed all over me," she said, giggling, "like a tomcat. So I left him to rest. I thought I'd clean up in the meantime. He's so hungry for me. Luckily, he's got stamina. It's nice to have a man like that, isn't it?" she added, "But you should know. Arman is strong—a man who loves sex," she paused her eyes heavenward, "a joy for a woman."

Aleese looked at Cisca curiously. "You two were lovers?" She felt Cisca's fingers back on her.

"Mm-mm, yes. Back when we first came to San Juan, we were together for a year. But it's all over now. Stand still so I can put this gel on you."

So surprised was Aleese by Cisca's revelation, she complied, letting Cisca smooth the gel over her breasts. It felt so good, Aleese relaxed against Cisca and let her massage the gel over her nipples. Despite her better judgment, she was swept into a place she'd never been. As Cisca's hand wandered lower over her ass cheeks and between her legs a warning light went off.

"Stop!" she protested, pulling away just as Arman walked in the door.

Aleese laughed at his expression before she realized she was totally nude. Hastily she covered her breasts from his admiring eyes.

With a splendid powerful body, a towel strung low around his hips, Arman would have made a perfect Roman God. He leaned against the wall, his eyes riveted on the two women.

Cisca let out a tiny eek when she noticed her sexy roommate. "Really, Arman. You should knock. We are entitled to some privacy."

"My intention was not to disturb, but to help."

Aleese stepped behind Cisca. "I don't need help," she said over Cisca's shoulder.

"No, she doesn't," Cisca agreed.

"I think she does." Arman strode up to the stall. "I brought you a fresh towel, Aleese."

"Nothing for me?" Cisca teased. "I guess I'll just go back to the room." She stepped out of the shower leaving Aleese behind.

Feeling a little exposed, Aleese hastily followed.

From the hallway, a male voice boomed. "Cisca, darling, where are you? Your Honey Bear is ready to share his…"

No one was more astounded by what he saw in the bathroom than Jack. His eyes took in the two nude females and then rested on the lean muscular body of Arman. "What the hell? A three-some and no one included me?"

"That's why it's a three-some," Arman said, his lips twitching. "If you were included, this would be a four-some." He handed the clean towel to Aleese, who hastily covered up. From the rack behind him, he took a towel and firmly wrapped Cisca, tucking the corner into her cleavage. In a low tone, he said to Aleese, "I'll meet you in the lounge." He glanced at Jack and Cisca. "I think Aleese would like to be alone," motioning them out. "Jamy here?"

Jack chortled. "We got rid of him a while ago. Sent him out for groceries. Come on, Cisca." He glanced at his watch. "We still have time."

Cisca glared at Arman. "This towel is nasty. You could have brought me a clean one, too." Dropping it on the floor, she stalked out.

Jack smiled apologetically. "Sorry, guys. I'd better go. Hey, don't do anything I wouldn't do." He swaggered into Cisco's bedroom after her. They heard laughter and a squeal.

Arman gave Aleese a last smoldering look before clicking the door shut behind him.

Left alone, Aleese had trouble sorting it all out. Through the process of drying her hair and applying her makeup, she wondered if she had somehow spoiled things with Arman. Well, she'd find out soon enough, she thought, slipping on her skirt and top. Arman had said he loved her in heels and that's what he'd get.

On the marble tile floor, her heels clicked as she made her way down the hall. She remembered the location of the lounge where the nude painting of Cisca graced the room. She had been struck at the warmth of the art. In order to paint something so sensual, the artist had to be a different sort of man.

Arman was stretched across a rather fancy gold velveteen couch, his legs hanging over the edge, his head resting on a pillow.

Approaching quietly, Aleese whispered, "Arman?" not sure if he was asleep.

He opened his eyes and smiled. "Ready for adventure?"

"Always."

"That's my woman." Swinging off the couch, he met her eyes. "I'm beginning to think you're an erotic goddess." He took her hand. "Let's go see the fort."

3

The fort was spectacular. Perched high on a cliff, the gray stone structure sparkled golden in the afternoon sunlight. They'd left the scooter parked at the bottom of the hill and trekked up on foot. Aleese was wondering if heels were the best choice, but with Arman holding her hand, she felt like she could climb a mountain.

"The Spaniards built the foundation in 1539, but it took another two hundred years to complete it."

"I've seen forts in Canada, but they're wooden." Aleese glanced up. "This one is huge."

"El Morro was built to protect against a sea attack." Approaching the gate, Arman said, "Over time, the Spaniards kept adding levels."

After he'd paid their entrance fee, Arman led her to the stone stairs. "I think we should start with the view."

"Yes, I'd like that."

"You go first, babe."

He didn't know what he was in for. Glancing over her shoulder, Aleese smiled smoothly as Arman focused on her hips, swinging seductively ahead of him. Though his sunglasses shaded his expression, his mouth turned up at the corners.

Aleese stopped to peer down at the sea. "I like the view."

"Yeah, it's amazing," Arman said, watching her. His arm wrapped around her waist, slipped a bit lower to her hip. "I hope Cisca didn't piss you off."

"She is a little odd."

"Jealous."

"Of us?"

He nodded.

"We hardly know each other."

"Yeah, but she can see the potential."

Aleese gazed up at his full lips and felt her nipples perk. Her bra was molded to support and lift her mounds—an enticing parcel for him to admire. The thin lining of her bra did nothing, however, to hide her body's reaction. She crossed her arms. "I feel sorry for Jamy."

Arman glanced at her with interest. "Jamy is a dreamer, but he'll see the reality of the situation eventually and learn by his mistake."

"It's easy enough to be misled." Aleese pondered her attraction for Arman. He was hotter than any man she'd ever met and different—the complete opposite to her boyfriend. Keith was nothing like Arman, but that could be a good thing. As an engineer, his job was hardly a frivolous one. And he was especially loyal to her. Although attractive to the ladies, he hadn't looked at another woman since they'd met.

She glanced at the black t-shirt that stretched tightly across Arman's powerful chest and could almost imagine him sexy as all-get-out in an American Airlines uniform. What woman wouldn't want to hook up with him? And would he resist? Someone should have given her a good kick in the head when she'd gotten involved with him. But they'd all tried, hadn't they? Emilio, Jack and Cisca. Now there was another thing—Cisca. What was her game? All this made Aleese rethink her interest in the man standing before her.

"What is it? Are you alright?"

"Of course, I am," she snapped, irritated with herself. Obviously, when he'd arrived in the bathroom wearing only a towel, he'd thought she'd be an easy hook-up. This date had been a stupid idea and she'd been an idiot to have let it get this far. Her stomach tightened into a knot. This was a ridiculous fix to be in. There was only one thing to do. She would give him the silent treatment. After a bit of that, he'd get the message and hurry to take her back to her hotel and she'd be back with Keith with no one the wiser.

Arman frowned at the rushing surf slamming the base of the cliff. "Fantastic."

Glancing down, Aleese was suddenly aware of the tremendous height of the wall. "It's spectacular," she agreed, awed by the sheer height. Forgetting her plan to shut him out, her curiosity took over. "How high up are we?"

"One hundred and forty feet." He pointed down at the arches below. "Those are corridors connecting the fort—there are numerous hidden passages."

"Have you ever found one?"

"More than one." He tilted her chin up. "Something's wrong. Tell me."

"There's nothing wrong," she said shortly. "Let's go!" Leading the way down the stairs, she was more than ever determined to finish her date with Arman and return to the hotel. Once she'd seen the fort, she'd go back and apologize to Keith for her temporary insanity.

From the other side of the courtyard a tour group was gathering. She paused to watch them. The guide was pointing up and motioning for the group to follow him. They were heading towards them. He stopped and started talking loudly about the Spanish Armada. His voice was high pitched and slightly annoying. That wouldn't have bothered her except for one thing. A man in the group resembled Keith. In fact, it was Keith.

The tour group was making a slow approach while the guide told them about Francis Drake's attack. He motioned for all of them to huddle closer as he relayed the story.

"Want to see the passageways?"

"Mm-mm." Aleese clutched Arman's hand and pulled him along to the nearest passageway. As they entered she gave a sigh of relief. Inside, the ceiling was so low Arman had to stoop to walk.

A tiny window opened to the courtyard. Aleese went on her tip toes to peek out but couldn't quite see anything. She tried to push herself up higher. Without asking her, Arman grabbed her by the hips and perched her on ledge in front of the window, sliding his hands down her legs.

"Thanks," she said, twisting around to see the tour group. Keith had his back to her, but it was definitely him.

It startled her when she felt Arman's tongue on her ankle. She shivered with the sensation and turned back. The dark waves of his hair brushed her legs as he kissed her calf and lingered on her thigh. "Arman," she breathed. No one had ever kissed her leg like that before. Her nipples hardened visibly through her top. "No, you shouldn't."

"Beautiful," he whispered, disregarding her words. His hands tenderly stroked her legs as his tongue feathered up her inner thighs.

From outside, a woman's laughter. She tensed momentarily at the sound, but the voices grew fainter and once more she was pulled into his magnetic force. She relaxed against the stone.

"I want to taste you," he said softly, before he burrowed his face into her panties. Shoving the lace to one side, his tongue licked the folds of her pussy under the flimsy material. Her body shivered with the contact.

What wicked words…but so arousing. Aleese squirmed in her excitement, knowing that place between her thighs was already wet . Would he enjoy her smell or would she repel him with her flavor?

Arman tugged on her lacy panties. "Lift up," he said his voice husky. Hypnotized by the golden lights in his whisky eyes she felt powerless to resist. The breeze cooled her steamy center as he slipped off the fabric. "I need to get at your sweet clit."

His voice and his thoughts excited her. Resistance was swiftly becoming a fading thought.

Gently, but firmly, he spread her legs wider and caressed her inner thighs with tiny butterfly kisses. "Let me give you pleasure."

Whatever conclusions she'd come to earlier about ending it with Arman, were lost the second his tongue teased the moist nub between her folds. Soft, gentle licks that sent her soaring high into sensuous world where reality no longer existed. Her breathing became ragged as he tantalized her, sucking and licking her over and around her throbbing clit.

Aleese tingled from his attention. Nectar released on her folds and her wet pussy twitched in anticipation. Her fingers wove through his thick wavy locks holding him in place. She floated on a billowy cloud of arousal—her need for pleasure taking over. With one hand, she slid over the smooth skin of her breasts. Two fingers rolled her nipple while Arman stroked her thighs and kissed the folds of her pussy. She cried out as his teeth nipped, yet her legs encircled his neck, pressed against tightly—pleasure mingling with pain.

Voices from outside startled Aleese. They were louder and nearer now. Her heart pounded. Any second the tour group would enter the passageway.

"Help me down!" In a panic, she stretched her arms out to Arman.

Arman lifted her off the ledge. "Come." Pushing her skirt down, he steered her in the direction of the entrance.

Aleese shook her head. "No, we can't go that way. I can't be seen."

He shot her a look, but led her down the corridor where it dead-ended. They could hear the group entering the passageway.

The tour group leader's voice echoed in the tunnel. "These passageways had many secret enclosures in case of an enemy attack."

Aleese panicked. Any second, Keith would see her with Arman and she would be destroyed. Nothing would salvage their relationship.

Smiling mysteriously, Arman placed his hand on a stone, pushing upwards. A portion of the wall shifted and revealed a small enclosure. "After you, babe."

Aleese stepped in with Arman behind her. The stone moved back into position and they were in cool darkness.

"Look," Arman whispered, shoving a metal slat aside to reveal a tiny peephole.

Aleese placed her eye close and peered out at the tour group. Keith seemed to be very friendly with a woman in the group, a rather voluptuous redhead. She couldn't believe it. He wasn't a philandering type, but then again, she had denied him sex last night and he liked it regularly. He hadn't been too pleased when she'd smacked him either. This could be his way of getting even.

She stared at the bosomy redhead. Her boobs were hanging out of her clingy low-cut tank, ready for a wardrobe malfunction. Aleese, on the other hand, selected tasteful tops that complimented her figure, revealing some cleavage, but not too much. As a petite woman, she wore miniskirts to show off her legs to full advantage. In contrast, this woman wore a long flowing skirt to her ankles. She wasn't his type, or had she pegged him incorrectly? Glancing down, Aleese noticed the woman's flip-flops. Were those practical enough for Keith?

Her suppositions came to a halt as Arman pulled her close to nuzzle her neck. His hand pushed her hair aside and his tongue traced the ridge of her ear, while his hand cupped her breast. He must have read her mind, because he slipped her strap down to access her soft mound. While his fingers lifted her breast, his thumb stroked her flesh until her nipple begged for his lips. This was not to be as she was not tall enough and the space allowed him so little access. But, undaunted by the circumstance, Arman wet his fingers and caressed her hardening nubs.

The tour guide was taking his own sweet time talking about the stones used in construction. "These walls are five point five meters thick."

"Jorge, when did the construction take place?" Keith called out.

"Most was done during the 1760's, *señor*." The guide raised his voice. "You also might find it interesting that the towers are forty-four meters above sea level. Now, some of you gentlemen wanted some details about the war..."

He blathered on about the governor's predicament during the war. Which war? Aleese didn't care, not when Arman was making her drip with his touch. In the confines of his jeans, his cock felt hard as a rock, pressing against her. She leaned back and closed her eyes, more conscious than ever how her pussy tingled. Reaching behind her, through the jean material, she fondled his rod. She wanted so much to pull his zipper down and grip his erect member, making it her very own toy, but the space they were in was too tight for any comfortable satisfying sex.

Arman let go of her to lift her skirt, his long fingers finding her throbbing centre, once again. He dipped into the wet juice from her pussy before he located her folds and slid his finger up and down until she squirmed in her willingness to receive more pleasure.

"Spread your legs," he whispered in her ear.

Aleese brought her hand to her mouth to block the moan that escaped her lips. Oh, what she wouldn't give to have him inside of her, but if that was not to be, she needed sweet release. She wanted to come so badly, her body trembled.

"Folks, I'll be showing you the other passageway on the way to the barracks and then I'm afraid our tour is over. The gift shop is open another ten minutes before the fort closes today. If you have any further questions, I will be available at the exit. Thank you for visiting Fuerte San Felip del Morro, San Juan's most famous fort and the largest fort in the Caribbean."

The tour group gave him a round of applause and started to plod back to the courtyard.

Cool though it was in the stone enclosure, droplets of sweat trickled down the valley between her breasts. Her whole body was wet. Even the hair at the nape of her neck felt damp. Aleese brought her hand back to her swollen nipple and played with it as she leaned back against Arman's strong warm chest. Tilting her pelvis, she tried to make it easier for him to access her slit. His fingers knew what she wanted.

"Aleese."

"Yes-ss..."

"I'm going to make you come."

Rhythmically his fingers worked her pussy, in and out, and up again to her clit, his fingertips wiggling inside her. When she heard the stragglers shuffling away, she allowed a suppressed groan to leave her lips. "Arman..."

"Aleese," he said hoarsely, "I can't get enough of you."

As his wet finger pressed between the folds to pulse her clit, Aleese felt a wave of overwhelming pleasure. Her thighs squeezed his hand in excitement, but he didn't stop. Tightened pelvic muscles and the continuous stroking pushed her into a place of no return. Heart racing, legs vibrating, her tortured scream muffled in the thick enclosure.

Aleese would have sunk down in a heap, zapped of all her energy, but the cold hard floor in the hidden passage was hardly the place.

"Was it good, babe?"

"Uh-hmm," she answered weakly, not sure she could formulate a coherent thought, "yes, very much. Thank you."

He took her face in his hands and kissed her lips in reply.

From her bag, a familiar melody sounded.

"Your phone."

It had to be Keith. "We'd better go, Arman. They're closing."

Placing his hand on a stone, he pushed and the wall moved. Sunlight greeted them once again.

Aleese's legs felt wobbly as they made their way to the entrance. She'd done exactly what she wanted to avoid, but it was out of her control. Arman was irresistible—like chocolate.

"Wait a sec," she said at the gate. "I should check my phone." Tugging it out of her bag, she found she had a text message waiting.

Dinner at 7 see u at the lobby

Keith. Aleese had no choice. This was it. She had to end it with one of them. Yet, there was no denying Arman was one smoking hot man who had given her the most tremendous orgasm of her life. But he only wanted her for sex, didn't he? He'd be fine without her. A guy like that could have another woman tomorrow. She frowned. And with that sex-kitten living in the house, it could happen tonight.

When Arman took her hand, a knot formed in her stomach. It didn't feel right to be two-timing either man.

Back at the scooter, Arman gave her a look. "Everything alright?"

"I need to get back to my hotel. Would you drive me there?"

"Of course. You need to get back now?" His eyes sent her undeniable messages.

Lying didn't come easily to Aleese. The sunglasses were a helpful mask. "I'm afraid my friend is in trouble. We're getting together for dinner."

"Would you like to get together for a drink afterwards?"

She hadn't expected him to be so persistent. "Probably can't leave her. She's very fragile right now."

Arman rubbed his lip thoughtfully as they reached the scooter. "Let me give you my cell number. That way if things change you can contact me." He held out a business card. Aleese took it and stuck it in her skirt pocket.

Slowly, he ran his fingertips down her cheek. "It was a special day."

More than she had ever imagined. Unforgettable. "Thank you for showing me the fort."

"I'm afraid I wasn't a very good guide, but it wasn't my fault. You distracted me, goddess."

Aleese blushed. "I shouldn't have."

"It was all beautiful." He kissed her lips lightly. "Nothing to be ashamed of. You're a very sensuous woman."

Aleese didn't know what to say. Arman took her tote and tossed it in the carrier. On the scooter, he grinned wickedly. "If you want to see more…of the island, that is, I'm here for the next few days, just a call away."

Aleese nodded slightly as she got on behind him. "Sure."

* * * *

Arman was not convinced. Revving the motor, he pulled out

onto the main drag. There had been no mention of a friend before. And at the fort, Aleese had avoided being seen by someone. Had it been this mysterious friend? There could be no reason to hide that. It was a cover-up—a lie. Putting two and two together, he came up with four. Aleese was married and the person she wanted to avoid in the tour group was her husband. He grimaced at his stupidity. *She played me.*

There was no denying Aleese was hot, but sex was sex, and if she didn't want more, that was her loss. With the scooter bringing him farther away from the hotel, he focused on putting Aleese out of his mind.

As he eased the bike up the hill, he found his thoughts wandering back to the passageway—the intense expression on her face when he'd first started to kiss her calf. In her excitement, she'd licked those pouty lips of hers. She had a mouth he could devour. And how she had sighed with each stroke of his hands on her lovely legs. Something she hadn't experienced before...he was sure. Aleese was a paradox—sweetly innocent and yet very sexual. No doubt about that. Back there in the fort, he should have fucked her. How sweet it would have been. His cock hardened as he thought about his fingers in her wet pussy. The mechanics of it would have been complicated, but manageable, had the fort remained open. The excitement of discovery had fired his lust and if he was not mistaken, hers. She intrigued him—unexplored, but open to all possibilities.

His mind bounced back to the first time he'd seen her nude. A luscious goddess yet so unconscious of her beauty. He'd had the impression no one had ever shown her the adoration she was due. She had been caught so unaware when he'd licked his way to her hot wet pussy. Smiling, he recalled Cisca's eager ministrations to Aleese's shapely body. In hindsight, he shouldn't have left her alone. Cisca was a carnivore...quick to leap on her prey. It was not beyond possibility that she could tempt Aleese. A sexual woman such as Aleese would be very curious.

Rounding the bend, he slowed down and rolled to a stop. He glanced down, his hard-on evident in his jeans. He shrugged his shoulders. If he didn't stop thinking about Aleese, he'd have do something about his hard dick. Pleasuring himself was not the most desired option, but his body didn't want to wait for that lying woman to come back for more. Getting off his bike he made his way to the door. Through the window he heard raised voices.

"You two are going without me? You ungrateful peon! Last night was the thrill of your life and now you…"

"Stop, Cisca! It's not like that, Sunshine. This is business. They wanted us to pose for the magazine spread. I promise I'll be back. Jamy can party after the shoot without me. I'll take you out for dinner."

A silence followed, at which, Arman quietly entered the hallway.

Cisca's head peaked around the corner. "Arman's home, guys." She indicated with her chin to Jack and Jamy who had joined her. "These two are off to model their wares for GQ."

"Lucky bastards. How did they get a hold of you?" Arman asked puzzled.

Jack grinned widely. "Jamy has connections. He dated the photographer."

"They're doing an article on men in uniform," Jamy added, gazing adoringly at Jack.

"Have fun!" Arman slapped Jack's hand as they passed.

Closing the door with his foot, Arman turned to Cisca. "How's it going with Jack?"

She grinned. "Couldn't be better. Poor Jamy. Sure he's won this one, but not for long. Jack is crazy about me." Her gaze dropped to the bulge in his pants. "Wow! I didn't know I still turned you on." Bringing her fingers down to his jeans, she asked, "Want some help with that?"

Arman shoved her hand away. "No thanks, Cisca. It's over, remember?"

Smiling slyly, Cisca watched as he strode over to his bedroom. Once inside, he locked the door.

Kicking off his slip-ons, he lay back on the bed trying to put some perceptive on the Aleese situation. Unconsciously, his hand wandered to his erection that threatened to burst out of his jeans. Uncomfortably tight. He unzipped his pants and allowed his cock to spring free. He glanced down at his stiff penis. Ever since he'd seen her, he'd gone around in a state of semi-arousal. The woman was capable of driving him over the edge. The wicked look in her eyes made him wild with lust.

Arman reached over to the lotion on his bedside table and squeezed some on his hands before he brought them back to his cock. Her skin was silky-smooth—so touchable. In his mind, he could visualize her nude in his arms. She was a goddess in every way—beautiful breasts that perked at the touch of his hand, a tight curvaceous ass that begged to be squeezed and lovely legs meant to be wrapped around him.

What a kiss—that tantalizing tongue provoking him until he had to have her. Beneath her shy exterior, Aleese was a wildcat who longed to have a tiger mate. Holding his throbbing penis, he imagined Aleese stroking him. She knew how much that would arouse him. Her pouty lips belonged on his rod, licking the head and caressing the shaft with her tongue. Her beautiful hands would smooth over his balls lovingly, kissing and nibbling till he couldn't take the teasing anymore. She'd prolong the agony with little licks on the head until she finally took him into her mouth.

Arman could feel his rod move in his hands as he stroked it with his fingertips. Pearly juice coated his hands while he fondled himself. She'd take him deep into her slippery cave. His dick sprung into its own tempo as his hands glided along the shaft. Squeezing his member for more impact, his pleasure increased with thoughts of the pressure of her lips on his dick. She would tighten her mouth around his cock until it moved with a life of its own, excited by the velvety soft wetness of her.

Propelled into the dream-like fantasy, he felt himself lose control. Slapping his rock-hard dick lightly, he closed his eyes, letting his fingertips work rhythmically up and down. She'd take him deep. Thrusting his cock steadily, he imagined Aleese mouth, wet and tight. From somewhere beyond, he heard a groan that came from a place deep within his body. His juices shot out. With the vision of Aleese swallowing his cum, his cock jerked repeatedly.

With another long groan, it all ended and his swollen member stood at half mast, still having memories of a woman that drove him insane with desire. He gazed down at his cock that refused to grow flaccid. Stirring restlessly, he sat up. If he thought about her any more he'd get another hard-on. A cold shower might help. It would be futile for him to wait for her call. He had to face up to the fact that she'd lied all along and he'd been played. It was time to forget her.

Dropping his clothes on a chair, he tugged on a robe before he opened the door. He was halfway down the hall when he heard Jack call out from the other bedroom, "Arman, we're heading out for dinner and the casino. Want to come?"

"When?"

"Soon, man." Jack poked out his head. "You can take that hot babe with you. What's her name?"

"Aleese," Arman said softly. He shook his head. "No, I doubt if she's available, but you can count me in." He eyed Jack curiously. "I thought you'd be at the photo shoot?"

"Things got screwed up. GQ wanted a sexy female flight attendant in the shoot, so I suggested Cisca. Was Jamy ever pissed when the photographer went for it. Anyway, I told him we'd do it tomorrow. Tonight, we're all available for dinner and the casino."

Arman smiled. "I think you made Cisca a happy woman."

Jack smirked. "Think she'll be grateful?" He punched Arman's shoulder. "You take the shower, man. See you in about an hour, 'kay?"

That's what he needed. A non-pressure evening with friends. Aleese was history.

4

At the table, Keith stared at Aleese, a forkful of sirloin poised at his lips. Suddenly, he chuckled appreciatively. "You had me going there, Aleese, but having a difference of opinion is hardly a reason to break up. That would be immature of us."

"It would be, but..."

He whispered, "I know what the problem is. Don't be embarrassed, honey. It's that time of the month, isn't it?" He poured some wine into her glass. "Drink up. I'll let you watch me play poker tonight. That should help that depressed mood of yours. You can be my lucky charm." Grinning widely, he added, "Not that I needed luck last night. I had that game in the palm of my hand. Did I tell you I made enough to pay for my vacation and then some?" He smiled slyly, "If you're a good little girl, and please Uncle Keith, I'll splurge and cover your hotel costs."

Not meeting his eyes, she picked at her steak. It was tender, but she'd lost her appetite. "I didn't mean to hit you, last night. I'm sorry, Keith."

"And you should be. There was no need to get violent, was there? I can't say I appreciated you rejecting me, either, but now that you've explained, I understand. You know those mood swings of yours are deadly." He cut into his steak. "Now this is dinner. Puerto Rican food is usually so lousy, but this is just like home." He glanced up. "Isn't yours done right? You're not eating much."

"My stomach is upset."

"Oh. You mean because of your female problems?"

Aleese nodded. The plan had been to end it with Arman, but her gut feeling was to do the reverse...break up with Keith.

Keith glanced in the direction of the bar. "If you'd rather not go to the casino, you could always lay down in the room."

Following his eyes, Aleese noticed a group of women, one of them the voluptuous redhead from the afternoon. So, he hadn't forgotten about her. From the way she was tossing her hair back, Aleese could see she was all too aware that Keith was watching.

Aleese sipped her wine contemplatively.

Keith wasn't the good guy he made himself out to be. With that massive ego of his, he couldn't even comprehend that she was trying to sever their relationship. But maybe she was being hasty. Keith did have a good job and a future, unlike Arman. Every woman needed security, especially if she wanted children. Not that Aleese was ready for any of that drudgery. She'd seen how her mother had bowed and scraped for her domineering father—a typical European male. In his mind, men were the hunters and women were there to do their bidding no matter if they had a career or not.

Inwardly, she abhorred traditional roles. There was no way she wanted to follow in her mother's footsteps as the hausfrau. At least, she had an education and a job. Teaching was a conservative profession, totally lacking in flamboyance, but with a salary came independence.

On the other hand, if she decided to keep on seeing Arman, she would have the most daring sex. She could see his potential. Spontaneity was his middle name. And she'd have the opportunity to see him again when she got home. A ground job might be a good thing. It could mean advancement and financial security. Arman was intelligent. He could go places. She smiled thinking how he'd be CEO of American Airlines in a few years.

Then, the reality of her situation struck her. Breaking up would be awkward. After all, she'd paid for her share of the room. And why should she leave? Why not Keith? There was no reason to feel guilty either. She glanced over at Keith whose eyes flitted to the bar in between mouthfuls of steak and potato. For all intents and purposes, they were even. Keith had his little flirtation with the redhead and she had the memory of Arman's exploring tongue— the orgasm of a lifetime.

But then her mind did an about-face. The fact that Keith suggested he'd pay for her hotel costs made her feel a trifle guilty. He was being unexpectedly generous. She really didn't deserve a boyfriend like him, did she? Pro and con arguments whirled about in her brain.

She needed space to figure this out. One thing was for sure, she wouldn't be able to split up with him and afford another hotel room. Certainly not in this hotel. Five more nights at two hundred dollars a night? Not even a possibility. She'd already blown too much on this trip. Aleese sighed. It wouldn't be easy to get herself out of this fix. It would be wise if she could stick it out with Keith for the rest of the trip. He had future potential. Arman's flight attendant job was as unreliable as an actor's.

Once in a Toronto club, Aleese had met one. All he wanted was a hookup. And with an actor, it was all about him. Same thing for flight attendants. They were like birds flitting from tree to tree— sailors with a girl in every port. As much as she tried, images of Arman's sensuous caresses jumbled her brain and wouldn't quit. He'd be difficult to forget, but she had no choice. Life wasn't all about sex. Arman wouldn't really be upset if she never called. He'd move on to some other woman within the week.

Watching Keith shovel in a potato, she casually remarked, "Keith, I'd really like to try a bit of gambling myself. Do you mind?"

He shot her a pained look. "It's up to you. But come watch me play poker afterwards. And, Aleese," he patted her hand paternally, "don't do anything foolish. It's all geared for the house to win, remember?"

"I just want to try it…for fun. I won't take that much money."

"Sure," his eyes flitted back to the bar, "why don't you get ready and I'll see you downstairs later." He snapped his fingers for a waiter.

Aleese placed her napkin on the table and headed out of the restaurant to the elevator.

When she arrived at the room, she inserted the card key into the slot and let herself in. A glance in the mirror told her the dress was way too dowdy for the casino. Teaching was a job. It shouldn't define her as a person. People always presumed teachers were something like ministers—staid, conservative and boring.

Aleese was different. Sure, she liked her job and the kids but she needed to have fun and someone to make her life complete. But that was wishful thinking—fantasy. She didn't really believe in love. There was no use getting tied down with a man. She had years before she needed to get serious about a relationship.

As she slid open the closet door, she recalled the touch of Arman's fingers as he smoothed the suntan lotion on her back. Had she flipped over, would Arman have continued his massage over her breasts? Recalling his sensuous touch, her hand crept under her neckline to the soft skin of her mound. His lips would caress her, pushing her to a point of no return.

She stroked her breast, her fingertips rolling her nub into hardness. She could imagine him taking it in his mouth. Closing her eyes, she fantasized his dark locks brushing against her erect nipple. But she forced herself to stop, knowing that the more she thought of Arman, the more her resolve to stay with Keith would diminish.

Aleese peered into the closet in search of a seductive dress— something a teacher should never wear. She found it. A clingy red dress with a low neckline.

With a lacy bra fastened, she searched for matching panties in the dresser. No, not tonight. Suddenly, feeling wicked, Aleese decided she'd go commando and feel the cool breeze between her thighs. No one would be the wiser.

Sexy, naughty thoughts of Arman surfaced—his shimmering dark eyes and those long fingers that touched her very fiber. His mouth would find her cleavage, his tongue licking the valley between her breasts until he could wait no longer. He'd pull the straps of her dress over her shoulders allowing her breasts to spill out. Her nipple would rise to his touch and wait for his sensuous lips to suck her into a state of bliss.

Aleese shook her head in frustration. Why was life so difficult? The reality was…she was stuck with Keith. Maybe she could forget about his ego and focus on his positive points. She frowned. But Arman was delicious and irresistible—like chocolate. It took all her will power to stop herself from calling his cell, but with a last glance in the mirror, she headed out the door.

Strutting into the busy casino, Aleese felt her self-confidence build as men swiveled in their chairs to watch her. She didn't mind the adoration of males. No, she'd had too little of that in her life— especially the last few months with Keith. Smiling, she walked over to a table putting aside all thoughts of men. For now, her game would be blackjack.

Standing behind a heavy man seated at the table, Aleese noticed his pinky ring as he tapped the table for another card—an impressive square-cut diamond. And as her eyes swept over to the woman seated next to him, Aleese decided she had chosen correctly when it came to her own gown. The older blonde at the table was chicly decked out in a sequined designer outfit, accessorized with a diamond necklace. As the big man stood up and took his chips, Aleese quickly moved aside. The dealer motioned for her to sit and this time, she did.

While he dealt the cards, Aleese recalled the rules. If she got a Blackjack it was an automatic win. That would mean a combination of a face card and an ace. Otherwise, she'd need to beat the dealer's total without going over twenty-one.

The first deal was easy. With a count of nineteen, it would be a risk to ask for another card. She waited anxiously for the dealer's last card. They totaled eighteen. She smiled with her sudden good fortune.

After the dealer laid down her winnings, Aleese felt a flush of excitement. It was a good sign. Her luck must be turning. Somehow, she'd get through this ordeal. Although, she wasn't entirely convinced she should break up with Keith, she was beginning to think she needed to be free again. She looked at her cards but the essence of her lover was imprinted on her unconscious mind. As she stared at the King of Hearts, she saw Arman—the King's dark hair and eyes became his.

Only when the waiter brought her a margarita, did Aleese finally relax enough to stop agonizing over which man to choose. Glancing around the casino at all the activity, she felt exhilarated that she was here in Puerto Rico and doing something new. For the next while, she focused on the game and though she lost a few times, she also won.

Knowing liquor hit her quickly, Aleese sipped her margarita cautiously before she checked her hand and tapped the table for another card. Feeling reckless, she signaled for another card even though her total was already eighteen. It would be worth the risk. When the three of spades turned up, her count totaled twenty-one. Aleese was ecstatic! There was now a pile of winnings.

At that moment the seat next to her was taken by a man in a dark jacket. Something familiar about his scent made her glance in the man's direction. When she turned to look, her jaw dropped. It was Arman!

He traded the dealer some money for chips. Oddly, he hadn't acknowledged her presence. Whatever game he was playing, she could play it, too. I'll be cool as a cucumber, she thought, leaning back in her chair. But her heart pounded so fiercely she was sure everyone at the table heard it. Perspiration gathered under her armpits wondering why he was acting so distant. Hesitantly, she glanced at him. Arman ignored her, his attention on the dealer. His arresting profile made her tingle, but when she saw his mouth drawn tightly, she concluded he was angry with her. When he continued to disregard her, she bit her lip in annoyance. But Aleese never gave up easily. She was determined to be noticed. Slyly, she slid her foot up and then down his leg. By the sudden look he shot her, she knew she had succeeded in catching his attention.

"Hi," she whispered huskily. She parted her mouth and ran a finger over her full lips. Arman had trouble looking away, his eyes fixed on her pouty mouth.

The dealer coughed, discretely drawing their attention back to the game.

Five, four, seven lay on the table in front of her. She nodded distractedly, and glanced back at Arman's sensuous lips. When the dealer turned up another seven, she realized her mistake. Twenty-three. Her eyes on Arman's long fingers, she watched him tap the table and once again, until his cards totaled twenty.

Aware that he was watching her, Aleese ran her fingers down her halter top, trailed them to the v-neck of her gown, and when they reached her deep cleavage she lightly skimmed her breasts. Arman's eyelids grew heavy, his whiskey eyes glimmering golden.

Aleese smiled slightly, pleased at his response, but she wanted more. Could she distract him from the game? While she kept her eyes on the dealer, she reached under the table and placed her hand on Arman's leg. It was muscular and hard, just like a man's body should be. She massaged his thigh. Arman leaned back in his chair. A wave of dark hair brushed his forehead making him look particularly roguish. He was a very sexy man, Aleese thought. She must have been out of her mind to think Keith was the one for her. Slowly, she brought her hand up to his crotch.

Glancing sidelong, she could see his changing expression, his mouth turning up at the corners, ever so slightly. With her fingers she circled around coming increasing closer to his member. She watched Arman shift uncomfortably. Did he have an erection? Aleese smiled at the thought. Soon she'd find out.

Tantalizing him thrilled her, but when she saw his enigmatic eyes burn with a fierce inner fire, Aleese faltered. All further thoughts of teasing him were lost. She desperately needed to touch him. Through the thin material of his dress pants, she felt his swollen rod. Slowly, she slid her hand, conscious of the power she had—the special strength a woman has when a man is aroused for her. When she squeezed his magnificent member tenderly, he gazed at her, the heat in his body reflected in his eyes.

Strangely, caressing him like this, made her more aware of their connection. Confused by this new insight, she let her fingers flow over his bulge again, her hand fondling playfully. If only she could enter his mind and read his thoughts. Did Arman feel this special magic she hesitated to even acknowledge to herself?

Bringing her attention back to the game, she watched the dealer and his exchange with the lady on Arman's right, and she waited. The dealer dealt his last card—totaling nineteen. It was a payoff for Arman, but a loss for her.

Reluctantly, she withdrew her hand and moved her chip into place for the next deal. Sitting back in her chair, she reflected how Arman still wanted her. His body couldn't lie. Was he thinking of the fort and their sizzling encounter? Aleese felt tingles in her core thinking of his hands and lips all over her and finally, that very intense orgasm.

Lost in a memory of his head between her thighs, hair brushing bare tender skin, she was suddenly thrown back to reality as a blast of cool air shot out from a vent below. Aleese shivered. Reaching under the table her skirt had hiked up to her thighs. No wonder she was cold. Aleese gripped the material and tugged.

But she was not the only one concerned. Before it dawned on her what was happening, Arman's large hand landed on her knee and long fingers slid up under the silk to her inner thighs, where they lingered. Stunned, Aleese waited. Lightly stroking her velvety skin, the hand slid higher until his search ended with a discovery— the soft folds of her pussy. She caught the look of surprise in his eyes at her pantyless state before they flashed back to the dealer.

In the midst of Arman's exploration, the game continued. The dealer turned up the Jack of Spades, staring challengingly back at Aleese with one dark eye. The others were dealt their cards and lastly, the dealer turned up the King of Spades for himself.

It was surreal. Aleese could hardly believe where Arman's wandering finger was going. Electricity sparked her core. Squirming in her chair, she felt powerless to resist. He reached between her legs and she willingly parted her thighs allowing him access. His finger smoothed over the silken folds to the moist lips before finding her swollen button. Greedily, she pushed her pelvis against his hand, fearful he'd take away her pleasure. But Arman had no intention of withdrawing, a finger stroking lightly over her throbbing clit with just the right amount of pressure and tempo. She was plunged into a sensual ocean—waves of pleasure plummeting her center. Her thoughts were only of her need for Arman and his pleasuring finger. Wiggling restlessly, she tried to control herself before anyone else at the table noticed. A hand to her mouth and all her will power suppressed the inevitable moan.

In a dreamy haze, the Blackjack game seemed like a drug-induced hallucination. She was vaguely aware of the dealer's questioning look. Given no direction, the dealer turned up an ace. Aleese glued her eyes on her final card.

From behind her, she heard a chuckle. A familiar squeeze to her shoulder—Keith stooped down and whispered in her ear. "Good gracious, Aleese. You did it—a Blackjack. You are doing well, aren't you?" He stood there watching as she was dealt another hand.

When she failed to place her bet, he picked up a chip, and plopped it down. "There, we go," he said and shot her a look. "You are out of it, Aleese." He glanced at her margarita. "I think you've had enough, wouldn't you say?"

Why was Keith here? Aleese jerked as Arman inserted his fingertips inside the mouth of her pulsing pussy. She was already so wet the added stimulus surged inside her like wildfire. This new sensation was so delicious she temporarily tuned out Keith.

"Hold on sixteen, Aleese," he ordered sharply. When she didn't respond, he persisted, "You are in no condition to play. I know how alcohol affects you."

Heat rose to her cheeks, in her embarrassment. She glanced at Arman. His amber eyes examined her coolly. He knew that Keith was her boyfriend. It was no surprise to Aleese when his fingertips withdrew. Arman was furious with her.

The dealer coughed discreetly, bringing her attention back to the game. Arman's first card was the Queen of Hearts. An ace came up next. Aleese's heart skipped a beat. A blackjack for him. When the dealer bust, chips piled up for them both. Lucky in cards, unlucky in love, Aleese surmised. The dealer dealt the next hand. Unexpectedly, Arman's finger returned to the soft folds of her v-zone, finding her aroused clit.

The dealer raised his eyebrow. After the second card appeared, Keith advised, "You need to split your nines, Aleese."

"Mm-mm," she murmured breathlessly, her clit throbbing uncontrollably. She had no idea what he was talking about and was way too far gone to care.

"Split?" the dealer asked.

Aleese nodded, not entirely sure of what she was agreeing to, caught up in the clean citron scent of Arman that lingered in the air. Her selfish pussy longed for his fingers. She sighed loudly, overpowered by her desire.

"Aleese, this is your last hand," Keith said decisively. "I think you need some rest." Keith had decided the combination of a margarita and hormone fluctuations had done her in.

So swept up was she in the sweet sensations of Arman's finger stroking her needy nub, Aleese tuned him out. She could only focus on Arman. But were her flushed face and steamy body giving her away? Surely her sighs didn't go unnoticed? Glancing down, she was relieved to see her dress hid her stiffening nipples. As she tilted her head to Arman, Aleese could see the heat in the golden depths of his eyes.

Increasing the pressure, he quickened the pace until the room spun and danced before her. Delirious from his touch, she frantically pushed against him, her pussy contracting with each probing thrust of his fingers. Arman's outrageous spirit was contagious. Aleese was drawn into something that she couldn't get out of, nor did she want to.

"Aleese," Keith said authoritatively, pulling her up, "come on! We're going. Take your chips. You need to lie down. You are obviously not well."

5

Arman watched her go. He couldn't believe what had just happened. Where was his brain? With her boyfriend standing behind her chair, he had made Aleese come. He should have gotten up then and there and joined Jack at the poker table, but the more he looked at that temptress the more he wanted to touch her.

If she hadn't brought his attention to the beauty of her breasts or her pouty mouth, he could have ignored her. True, not for long, but he did have some will power although maybe his dick wasn't quite as determined. The second he'd seen her tonight, he'd felt stirrings. Beside her, he'd become rock-hard. And when those smooth, velvety thighs parted so easily for him to stroke—she was a wet dream come to life. It was all crazy, but why should he stop something they both wanted? That was a boyfriend not her husband—unless he was mistaken about the lack of rings.

But he couldn't absolve the woman. What was the story here? Abruptly, he rose from the table and spying Jamy at the doorway, strode over to his roommate.

"What's up?" Jamy asked, noting Arman's brooding expression.

"I'm leaving. I've had enough. Might as well go home."

Jamy raised an eyebrow.

"Lost too much?"

"You could say that. It's just not my night."

Jamy patted his shoulder. "I saw you with Aleese. It didn't go well?'

"She's lied to me."

"About?"

"She came on this trip with her boyfriend."

Jamy shrugged his shoulders. "Boyfriends come and go."

Arman looked at Jamy with concern. "You and Jack?"

"Yeah, we're finished." He brightened. "But as Scarlett said…tomorrow is another day."

"You mean—you've found someone else, already?"

Jamy grinned. "Rediscovered. Remember the GQ shoot?"

Arman nodded.

"The photographer," Jamy said, "still has a thing for me and," he smiled, "he was kind of special."

"That's great. So you and Jack?"

"Finished. He loves Cisca. Can you believe it?"

Arman shook his head. "Love is a mystery."

"Want to split cab fare?"

Arman nodded. "Depending if you're going home."

"Yep. Need to be up bright and bushy-tailed tomorrow for the shoot anyway." He patted his face. "Don't want shadows to ruin this handsome visage."

They walked over to the entrance. The doorman whistled for a cab and they got in when the first one pulled up. Jamy gave the driver the address. "So, this is the end for you and Aleese?"

"Yeah. She made up her mind when she walked out with him." Arman stared straight ahead.

Knowing his friend was not feeling too sociable, Jamy patted his arm understandingly. Along the ride home, he chatted with the cabby as they drove slowly on the busy boulevard.

Arman sat back in his seat and tried to think of other things, but the image of Aleese's lovely face wouldn't disappear. The street lights became her dazzling blue eyes. The warm humid air blowing in from the open windows reminded him of the motor bike ride and how her blonde hair had flown wildly around her face. Watching the palms wave in the wind, he saw her lithe body dancing in front of him.

When they arrived at the house, Jamy frowned, studying Arman's expression. "Hey, man. You take it easy, okay? Things have a way of working out for the better. Aleese is a hot babe, but there are plenty of fish in the sea."

"Yeah, I know," Arman said, but growled softly, "just not like her."

When Jamy said goodnight, Arman was left alone to stew. Shot down again. For some reason, the goddess preferred that overbearing bastard.

Arman grabbed a bottle of scotch off the table and poured himself a dram. From the decanter, he added a splash of water and then seated himself on the living room couch, feet up on the coffee table. He studied the hue of the scotch before he swung back his glass, downing most of it in one slug.

It burned going down—powerful enough to numb his emotions. After that one, he had another and he was ready for a third except reason stepped in. Drinking wasn't the solution—another woman was. Which woman? There were plenty, as Jamy had said. Soon Aleese would become a distant memory or a bad dream.

6

Keith left Aleese and went back down to the casino. He had insisted she go to bed, but the stress she felt made this impossible. On her way out, she'd glanced back at the Blackjack table. In Arman's dark eyes there was only betrayal and sadness. He had searched for answers and she'd run away like the coward she was.

Vigorously, Aleese punched her pillow in her frustration. It was her fault. When she screwed up, she did it royally. It wasn't fair the way she'd treated him. She had to make it right with Arman. Tomorrow, she promised herself. And having made that decision, she relaxed enough to drift into an uneasy sleep.

In the morning, it was no surprise to Aleese to find Keith gone. He had a tendency to be an early bird. When she got up she found out where. A note was on the bedside table.

Going out with some friends I met yesterday. Text me if you want to get together later. K

So Keith had decided there was no use spending time with her if she had her period? Come to think of it, hadn't he always found something else to do when he knew they couldn't have sex? Her cycle lasted five days. Did that mean he'd be occupied for the rest of their vacation? She smiled. This was convenient. There was no way he'd be making sexual demands on her. He hadn't even made definite plans for tonight. Well, this was to her advantage, she thought—an opportunity to see Arman without any interference from Keith.

After a quick shower, Aleese got ready and left the room. On the elevator going down she glanced at her sundress—a bright yellow with an A-line skirt, a woven scarf around her waist and heeled nude sandals to give her legs that extra long look. She'd outdone herself. The long white feather earrings were edgy enough to attract a man like Arman. He'd be hot for her—if not crazy with lust.

With a surefire plan, she felt confident she could persuade Arman to forgive her. If only she could find that pretty little house—the white stucco bungalow, a red tile roof and a bougainvillea tree at the iron gate. She'd catch a taxi and hope she could remember where it was. There was no point in trying his cell. With the look he'd given her yesterday, she'd be lucky if he ever spoke to her again.

But first, she needed to stop by the gift shop. They had chocolates. She was sure she had spotted some the first day they had arrived. Unfortunately, Keith had urged her to continue on up to the room for his version of dessert. Regretfully, she had gone, but not today.

"*Buenos dias, señorita,*" the fashionable Latina smiled in welcome. "What can I help you with?"

"I'm looking for chocolates."

"Yes, of course. We have several varieties." She led the way to a multi-tiered counter and got behind it. Each level had an assortment of truffles.

"Ah-hh," Aleese sighed, spotting milk-chocolate candies. Although she didn't like dark, she thought Arman might. "I can select which ones I want?"

The lady nodded. "A small box?" She held up a box for eight chocolate truffles.

"Yes. That's perfect." Aleese pointed to a strawberry-filled milk chocolate truffle and a mocha hazelnut in a dark chocolate shell. "Four of each, please."

She watched as the lady prepared the box and placed a golden lid on top. If he really did like chocolate, this was the perfect gift. This would be on top of the other treats she had in store for him. He'd have to forgive her. She couldn't imagine staying angry at someone bearing chocolate truffles—such creamy, deliciously sinful ones.

Having accomplished part of her mission, it was up to her to find a taxi with an astute driver. At the front of the hotel, a taxi waited.

"*Hola,*" she called out to the driver in the waiting cab. "Are you free?"

"Yes." The man got out. "Where to, *señorita?*" he asked, opening the door for her.

"Well, that's a bit of a problem but," Aleese said hesitantly, getting into the back seat, "I'm sure you can figure it out."

The taxi driver looked back in puzzlement over his shoulder.

"You mean I should just drive around and show you the sites of San Juan?" He started the engine and waited at the junction of the circular driveway and the street.

"No, not exactly. I want you to find a house. Turn right."

"Alright." The taxi swerved onto the street. "Now what?"

"We need to drive to the old town."

They made their way slowly through the busy traffic. Aleese grew more nervous as they approached. Once on the cobblestone street, she knew they were close to the house. What should she say? Would he understand? She had always thought she needed a practical, financially-secure man like Keith, but she'd found out her heart wasn't there. Arman was different from any man she'd met. He was the one who intrigued her.

Noticing they had passed the café where she had met Arman, she looked for the street they had taken after their visit to the beach. "Go past that shop," she said quickly, "and turn just ahead."

The driver nodded. Following her directions, he made a right and drove up a residential street. Pale aqua, green and yellow houses dotted amongst the white stucco homes.

"Slow down now, please. It's further up this hill, I remember. We're looking for a white stucco house with a red-tiled roof. There's a bougainvillea tree at the gate."

The driver chortled. "Plenty of houses like that *señorita*. It's the Spanish style common here in Puerto Rico."

"I know it won't be easy, but I'm sure I'll recognize it."

"*Si*," he said doubtfully, driving at a snail's pace up the steep cobble-stoned hill.

There were several white stucco houses—all attractive with either hibiscus or bougainvillea trees but she remembered Arman's house had a black wrought-iron fence and the tree had purple flowers. Suddenly, she spotted it.

"There it is!" She pointed excitedly. "Stop here."

After paying the driver, Aleese stood uncertainly at the gate. This was *mission impossible*. Arman might not even speak to her, let alone forgive her. She almost gave up, but leaving would be cowardly. If she didn't try to explain why she hadn't told him now, she would kick herself for losing a man who spiked her passions in a way no one had before. This was her one chance. There might never be another.

Her eyes swept the house for signs of activity and seeing none she unfastened the gate and trekked to the entrance. At the wide wooden door, she looked for a door bell and finding none, took hold of the brass knocker in the shape of a lion's head and clanged it against the oak. Not sure if it could be heard from within, she repeated the motion once more. Disappointed, she was about to leave in defeat when the door opened.

In thin cotton pajama bottoms and nothing else, Arman was nude to the waist—splendid broad shoulders, tight abs and narrow waist exposed to her view. Black hair was tousled alluringly, but his dark eyes were angry and his sensuous lips curled downwards at the corners. Before he could close the door in her face, Aleese ducked under his arm and stepped into the hallway.

"What are you doing here?" he asked coldly.

Put off by his hostility, Aleese stuttered uncertainly, "I...I had to come, Arman. Please listen to what I have to say."

Arman glowered at her. "I think you should go."

From the mirror behind him, Aleese could see the strong muscles in Arman's back. He was so striking, a current coursed through her body. Flustered, she glanced up at him, knowing her mission was futile. He had shut his heart to her.

Arman swung the door open. "Good bye."

Not one to give up easily, Aleese stubbornly took hold of the door and shoved it shut before she turned around to face him. "Hear me out. This is important. I'm really sorry, Arman. I should have told you about my situation."

"And then you think it would have been okay?"

Aleese placed one hand on his chest. "No, of course not. I...didn't mean..." The warmth of his skin was making it impossible for her to think straight.

"You thought it was all right to lie and lead me on while you continued to sleep with your boyfriend?"

She scraped her fingernails on the surface of his chest and ran them down to his abs, trying to frame her thoughts. "I started seeing Keith last summer. He was charming, witty and intelligent. I thought we were in love. We booked this holiday months ago. But a lot has happened since then. I began to get to know him better and I wasn't sure anymore. It was too late to cancel the trip and rebook it alone without a huge loss I couldn't afford. I thought

I could deal with Keith for one week, but when we got here I considered breaking it off—especially after we met."

"Why didn't you tell me this?"

"We had just met. I didn't know you well or you me. I was confused about what to do. Keith was still talking marriage and…"

"You wanted to marry him?" Arman said in disbelief.

Aleese shook her head. "At first. My friends are married or living together. I was beginning to believe I'd never find *the one*. I thought I should hurry and decide on a man with a good job and a future."

"And that would be Keith?"

Aleese shrugged.

"Rather calculating of you, isn't it?"

"My parents were immigrants, so I grew up without a lot. I worked hard to pay for university to be independent, but it's more complicated for a woman, especially if she hopes to have children one day. I wouldn't be the only one who considered security and stability. If I were pregnant, I would need that for my child. Even though I had a good job, I imagined once I had children it would depend more on my husband to support us." Aleese looked earnestly at Arman and gripped his arm. "And my parents thought Keith was right for me. I guess I started to believe them."

"So you lied to me."

"I should have told you right away, Arman." Aleese was getting distracted. Under her fingers, Arman's bicep was hard and powerful. She forced herself to continue. Apologetically, she said, "That was wrong of me. But I came here because I wanted you to know that I broke up with Keith."

"When?"

"After our visit to the fort. When we drove up, I told you I would be talking to a friend about a problem. That was kind of true. I decided at dinner to tell Keith we were over."

Arman laughed dryly. "You did? That must have been very successful. Is that why he was checking up on you at the casino later—because you broke up with him?"

"He couldn't believe I was serious." Aleese looked beseechingly up at Arman. "He thought I was in a lousy mood because of my period."

"You have your period?"

"No, he just assumed that because I was rejecting him." Aleese met his eyes. "He'd come in the night before—the night we'd met and I refused to have sex with him."

"Okay, but that doesn't explain why you didn't stay at the blackjack table with me. Instead, you let him drag you out of there."

"I wasn't thinking straight, Arman. You were touching me and I…"

He glared at her. "So it's my fault? Aleese, you could have taken me aside and explained." Arman gazed at her steadily and quietly commented, "Well, you've said what you wanted to say." He motioned to the door with his chin. "You can go now."

Abruptly, Aleese dropped her purse. It clanged on the marble tiles as the metal clasp hit the floor. Impulsively wrapping her arms around Arman's waist, she whispered throatily, "I'm so …" caressing his neck with tiny kisses, she journeyed down his chest until her mouth found his nipple, "…sorry." Her hands ran over the curve of his ass, squeezing his muscular cheeks as she flicked her tongue, teasing his nipple. She added, "You have to…" he growled softly as she brought her attention back to his nub and sucked it, "…forgive me."

Arman held her head close to his chest while she tantalized him with her licks. Lightly biting him, Aleese heard his quick intake of breath and a groan. His arms encircled her. Bringing her hands to his waistband, she loosened it and tugged the pants down over his hips. His abs received tender kisses before she licked her way lower.

"Sit down," Aleese said in her smoky voice. Arman sank powerlessly into the arm chair. Kneeling before him she took hold of his erect cock, one hand on his balls.

In the mirror, Arman watched Aleese as she licked and stroked his poker-stiff shaft. It was like seeing a porn movie and they were the stars. While his hands played in her fine blond hair, his rod ignited with her butterfly flicks. Heat welled up inside his cock, throbbing with every scorching caress. Arman could think of nothing but her sultry body. Undoing the ties at her neck, he watched the straps slowly slide off. Her dress fell to her waist, leaving a deep cleavage exposed by the low-cut lacy bra.

Arman smoothed his hands down the velvety skin of her back

and grasped her bra. Unhooking it, he pushed it down as far as it would go. Aleese shrugged it off and then arching her back, she thrust her breasts out. She was beautiful, he thought as he alternated between rolling her nipples and stroking her breasts. Everything about her was addictive.

But Arman needed more. He burned for her full lips to return to the head of his swollen rod and Aleese, almost as if she had read his mind, brought went down on her knees and took him in her mouth.

Whatever her crime was, he couldn't recall it anymore. He could only think of her lips pushing him into a steamy state of arousal. When his dick filled like a volcano on the brink of eruption, he gently pushed her face away and said huskily, "Stand up."

Eyes wide, she slowly got up to stand in front of him. Arman untied the scarf from her waist, letting it drop to the floor. With a push the dress loosened, sliding to the floor. She was naked save for silky stockings and lacy thong. The sight of her shapely legs in high-heels released a deep groan in Arman's throat.

From behind, the mirror reflected her curvaceous body. His eyes flicked to the woman before him. Aleese was a luscious goddess to be worshipped—every last inch of her. The roundness of her ass aroused him so much his recent anger became a blurry memory.

Arman scooped her firm cheeks into his hands, excited by the feel of her flesh under his fingers. With his hand, he brought her breast to his mouth and suckled her nipple. He felt her body shudder in response. With his other hand, he pushed under the thong and stroked the soft folds until he felt her juices well up. She pushed her pelvis against his hand and he knew he wanted her more than he'd ever wanted any woman.

Quickly, Arman swiveled Aleese around to face the large gilt-framed mirror. Her eyes were heavy-lidded with passion as he kissed her neck. When she arched against him, he pressed his lips to her shoulder while both hands slid around her slender waist. He glanced up to see Aleese stroking her breast while she stared into the mirror, her rapture at their movements evident in the glimmer of her turquoise eyes.

Watching her smooth her hands over a perfect mound, he said

softly, "Masturbate for me." To see her pleasure herself in the mirror while he played with her lovely breasts would be unbelievable. But would she?

Aleese's eyes glittered wickedly before she brought her hand to her clit. With her middle finger she lightly stroked, her eyes closed as if she were in a hypnotic trance.

Arman cupped her ripe breasts, fingering the hardened nipples while he watched her. Pressing against him, she moaned softly. The more he watched the more he was certain how insane he was to shove her out of his life. She was unlike any woman he had ever encountered—a paradox of sensuality and innocence.

His throbbing rod pressed against her smooth firm ass. His excitement was beyond belief. Seeing her in this euphoric state, he wanted to send her to a point of no return. He wanted her to beg for him so she would realize how much he meant to her. Aleese needed to know he was worth a thousand Keiths.

The anticipation built up inside him and his body ached for hers. Sweet pussy lips wet with nectar beckoned. Arman placed his hand between her legs. "Let me touch you now," he murmured in a low husky voice.

Aleese released her pussy to Arman's long sensitive fingers, allowing him to work his magic touch on her center. As her breathing became ragged with his strokes, he ventured to her slit. Was that his groan or had they both cried out as his fingers entered her hot wet pussy? She was ready and he would give it to her.

A narrow wooden table was directly below the mirror. Arman could see the possibilities. "Lean your hands on the table," he whispered, stepping out of his pants.

A lock of hair fell forward over her face as she steadied herself. From the mirror Aleese looked back—blue pools awakened with desire. As magnet attracts iron, Arman was drawn to her lithe body and her compelling beauty, wondering how she held this power over him. He knew he should take time to think. Could he ever trust her again? But thinking was no longer on his agenda—making love was. He had no inclination to resist her now. Arman moved in closer to the inviting curve of her ass and gripped his cock guiding it to the juicy entrance.

He would make this last, he thought. Cupping her ass cheeks, his cock teased, sliding against her. When he could hold out no longer, the tip of his throbbing rod surged forward.

The bang of the door and footsteps brought this action to a halt.

"Shit, Arman!" Jamy croaked in surprise. He shouted over his shoulder, "Wait, Jack! Um...Arman's in there."

"So?" Jack protested. "What the hell?"

"No!" Jamy shouted and turned around, blocking the entrance with his arm. "I'm serious, Jack! We can't go in. Arman has a woman with him." Discreetly, with his head turned away he muttered, "I'm so sorry Arman...Aleese...We'll wait. You just take your time."

Jack, however, wasn't so understanding. They could hear him berating Jamy. "This is stupid. We live here. I'm going in."

With lightening speed, Arman scooped up their clothes and, grabbing Aleese's hand, rushed her down the hall to his bedroom. When he slammed the door behind them, she looked so dazed he had to smile. With Jamy's shocked look fresh in his memory, his grin grew wider and he broke into a full-blown laugh.

Aleese stared at him in disbelief. "You are so...so evil," she stuttered, until she found herself replaying Jamy's arrival in her head and a giggle escaped. When she met Arman's twinkling eyes, she couldn't hold it back any longer—laughing as hard as Arman, she held her stomach to keep herself from bursting.

7

Their laugher barely died down when they heard a knock on the door.

"Arman, sorry to interrupt, but there's a message for you on voice mail. Urgent. Roger said to phone back as soon as you get it. Apparently, you haven't been answering your cell."

That had them both snickering again.

"I wonder why," Arman said to Aleese softly, a smile playing on his lips. "Thanks, Jamy!" he shouted back, before his eyes flicked to his cell lying on his bedside table. "Excuse me." He checked the number on his cell. "It's the manager."

He pressed a few buttons and listened intently before he clicked it off. Glancing at Aleese, a distant look on his face, he said, "They need me on the New York flight. I have to fill in. Apparently, the head purser is ill." Grabbing his watch from on top of his dresser, he pulled it on his wrist hurriedly, and said, "I have to go. I'm flying out in forty minutes."

"Oh," Aleese said, disappointed by his news. She'd been hopeful if they didn't continue that very hot sexual encounter at least he'd open up and she'd know how she stood. *Had he really forgiven her?* Reluctantly, she hooked the clasp of her bra and adjusted the straps while she watched Arman take his clothes from the closet.

As she picked up her dress, Arman's cell rang insistently.

"*Hola*, I can't speak to you right now. I have to get to the airport." Arman waited for the caller to talk. "Sure, that's nice of you, Shanna. Ten minutes?" From further snatches of conversation Aleese overheard, she got the impression someone was giving him a ride. When he said the woman's name again, Aleese began to feel a little insecure.

This was the end, then, she thought. He'd forgotten about her already. For him she was only a hook-up—disposable. Shanna was probably a girlfriend. Aleese frowned. Fate had thrown her a curve ball.

Distraught, Aleese was ready to admit defeat and leave.

Stepping into her dress, Aleese pulled it up and distractedly fastened the buttons. When she glanced over at Arman, she caught him staring at her. "What?'

"I don't know your room number."

"703—a room with a view," she said nervously. She thought how foolish she must sound chatting inanely about her room.

"I'll be there."

She paused, gripping her top button. "When?"

"Tonight, unless something goes wrong."

"But, I thought you'd be in New York?" Aleese said puzzled.

Arman pulled on his blue American Airlines jacket and picked up his carry-on. "It's not a layover. I'm back on the return flight. Will you be there at eight?"

Aleese couldn't take her eyes off of him—he was so sexy in his blue uniform. "I can be."

"We'll talk then. You ready to go?"

Aleese nodded. When he swung the door open for her, she preceded him down the hall, wishing she knew what he was thinking.

"Hey, Arman, you need a ride?" Jamy called out from the other room. "I'm leaving in awhile."

"No thanks, pal. Shanna is picking me up, but would you be able to drop off Aleese?"

Jamy popped out of the kitchen. "Sure," he said to Arman. "Hi, Aleese. Where're you going?"

"I'm staying at the Del Mar. I hope that's not out of your way? I could get a taxi if it's too much trouble."

Jamy shook his head. "No problem, if you're willing to wait. I'm making a salad. Want some?"

Aleese hadn't realized how hungry she was. Having skipped breakfast to get to Arman as soon as possible, she was ravenous. "That would be fantastic, Jamy. Are you sure it's not too much work."

"I'm sure. Gotta make something to eat anyway." He glanced at Arman. "Sorry about the interruption earlier, man. I had no idea."

Aleese blushed at his implication but Arman patted Jamy on the shoulder and grinned. "Don't worry about it." Turning back to her, Arman confirmed, "Room 703, at eight."

Aleese nodded and watched his tall lanky figure go down the

walkway to a waiting convertible where a pretty brunette waved from the driver's seat.

"Shanna," Jamy commented from over her shoulder, "she's cabin crew."

Aleese swung around and shot him a look. "Nothing personal, you mean?"

Jamy grinned. "Not that I know of." He took her elbow. "Come, Aleese. I think you need some nourishment. It'll help your energy level and clear your head. Are you okay with hard-boiled eggs and bacon bits on your salad?"

"You mean you think I'm getting paranoid?" she said, entering the spacious kitchen.

"What about tomatoes?"

She nodded.

"It's okay, Aleese. I'm a very understanding sort of fellow. You can talk to me." Indicating she should sit down at the heavy oak table, he rolled his eyes. "Heaven knows I've gone through enough grief with the men in my life." He wandered over to the counter and tossed the salad. "Pepper?" he asked, waving a pepper mill over the romaine and egg mixture.

"Thanks," she said quietly, wondering what Jamy could tell her without him going over the line as Arman's friend.

After Jamy sprinkled pepper on their salad, he placed plates and cutlery on the table along with some linen napkins. Carefully, he pushed them through silver napkin rings. "Aren't these cute? I found them in this little shop in the old town." He held one up for Aleese to examine. "See the birds?"

Aleese nodded. "Pretty. Are they seagulls?"

"Vultures I think."

"What? Really?"

"Quirky, eh?"

"I'll say." Aleese eyed Jamy suspiciously. "You were joking, weren't you?"

"Well, you were looking far too worried about the devastatingly enchanting Shanna and her plans for my charismatic roomy." He walked over to the counter and held up a bottle of wine. "Care for some Shiraz?"

"Shiraz. I love it. What kind do you have?"

"Yellow Tail, direct from Australia. Buddy of mine flies there.

Can't always get it here."

"What a coincidence. It's one of my favorites."

Jamy opened the cupboard door and took out two glasses. Filling them, he handed one over to her. "*Salud*," he said, clicking her glass.

Sitting down opposite her, Jamy glanced at Aleese and directed, "Let's eat and then you can tell me everything."

Aleese didn't protest. Good food always had a calming effect on her.

After they'd had a few sips of wine and a portion of salad, Jamy probed, "Alright, spill the beans, Aleese. What did you do that put Arman in that dark space last night?"

"Me?" she asked innocently.

"You were very naughty, weren't you?"

Aleese had visions of her hands all over Arman. Heat rose to her cheeks. "Well…"

Jamy raised his hands in protest and then laughed. "Just teasing, honey. No details necessary. After what I saw today, last night must have paled in comparison."

"I'm sorry, Jamy. I hadn't meant to go that far. He was so angry with me, I had to do something."

Forking in a mouthful of salad, he asked, "And you got him going, girl. I'd say you were very successful."

"If all he wanted is sex, yes. I was hoping you could clue me in about something else."

"Sure, what?"

"Does he have feelings for me, Jamy?"

Jamy refilled their glasses. "Arman doesn't talk about his emotions, Aleese. He's a guy, remember?"

Gazing at him over the rim of her glass, Aleese thought about his remark. She set down her glass. "He must have said something, Jamy. Think hard."

"Hm-mm. He was obviously upset about your boyfriend."

"I know he was. He told me I deceived him deliberately. It wasn't like that, Jamy. I admit. At first, I thought we'd have a fling and that would be it."

"You'd have been happy with that?'

"Arman is very sexy."

Jamy nodded understandingly. "You're not the first woman or

man, for that matter, to go crazy about Arman."

"Man?"

Jamy laughed. "No, unfortunately for us guys, he doesn't have inclinations in that direction."

"He's different from any man I've ever met."

"Apart from the fact that he's hotter than the spiciest tamale in Puerto Rico?"

"Mm-mm." In her mind, she visualized his sensuous lips and how he'd caressed her with that mouth until she had gone crazy with desire. "Arman's a free spirit. That's very attractive to me, especially after a year of dating Keith."

"Keith?"

"My engineer boyfriend. We came here on this vacation together."

"And you're still together and Arman is seething with jealousy."

"I doubt that. Arman was ready to throw me out today."

Jamy nodded for her to continue.

"I explained to him that I broke up with Keith."

"So, what's his problem then?"

"Keith didn't think we were finished. He couldn't comprehend how any lowly woman could possibly consider breaking up with someone as stupendous as him." Aleese waved her finger in the air. "That man's ego is colossal. And after I told him, he decided I was delusional. He said when I have hormonal mood swings I couldn't be taken seriously. So, I went into the casino to play blackjack and think the whole thing through before I phoned Arman. Unfortunately, the situation escalated out of proportion."

"Arman showed up at your table and you two played footsie?"

"Kind of."

"And then Keith the egomaniacal boyfriend joined you. Did they have words?"

Aleese shook her head. "Keith didn't have a clue that Arman and I were involved and I hadn't had a chance to explain it to Arman."

"Ah-hh!"

"Yes, you see how it was, except it got worse. Keith decided I was sloshed and took me back to the room."

"But you weren't."

"What?"

"Wasted."

"Well a bit. I really can't handle too much liquor and that margarita was huge." Aleese forked up an egg slice. "You see, that's what really got Arman angry." She added hastily, "Not me getting buzzed, but he thought I should have refused to go anywhere with Keith and I should have explained everything then and there."

"Difficult."

"You can say that again. I was so flustered. But when I tossed and turned in bed that night, worried that Arman would never forgive me, I had to take the chance and come and see him."

"Well, if it's really Arman you want, I think you played your cards right."

"Yes, I agree but…"

"What?"

"Arman is off to New York and he may decide when he's away, he doesn't like me enough to give us another chance. He called me a liar, Jamy, and he thought I was calculating."

"Why calculating?"

"Because I thought a man's job was important to a woman."

"And it is. The richer the man, the better his gifts." He held up his hand to show me his sapphire ring. "Got this from an oil man who thought I was the cutest thing he ever saw."

Aleese shook her head. "Money isn't the important thing, Jamy. Security is. I told him, there'd be a point when I'd have children. I won't be able to teach—full time, anyway. I tried to explain that to him. A woman wants a financially stable home for her children. At least that's the way women I work with think like. Maybe some women don't care, but I do. All my friends wanted a man with a job as well as one that isn't a druggie or alkie. He wouldn't have to be a professional, but he'd have to be a hardworking man I could be proud of."

Jamy nodded in agreement. "A guy who can protect and provide for his partner. I'm with you on that, Aleese. I'd give up flying any day and be a househusband. I want to adopt."

"Well, I'm not sure about marriage and children yet, but I guess I'd date guys that have potential. I'm not going to live the way my parents did—scraping and saving every penny. If that means never getting married, that's fine, too. I have a reasonable salary that will get better as I teach longer and if there isn't a man for me, I guess I'll settle for," she grinned, "sex with a hot man."

"Or hot sex with a hot man," Jamy agreed. He patted her hand. "You're funny, Aleese. I like you. Don't worry about Arman, he has to understand some people are more practical than he is. He thinks he's logical, but he has an imaginative side that is awesome. It can be a good thing when he starts working on his ground job. He'll be at the flight school teaching the course."

"Mm-mm." Aleese agreed. Never had her sex life been so exceptional—each experience surpassing the last. "Thanks for lunch, Jamy and the vote of confidence."

"You're okay, Aleese and unique yourself. It's not every woman that can keep up with him, but you've managed to." Jamy stacked the plates and brought them over to the counter. Aleese took their wine glasses.

"We'll leave them in the sink and head out, okay?" Jamy said.

Placing them in the sink, Aleese's hand slipped, knocking one over.

"Oopsy! Too much wine, honey?"

Aleese grinned. "Good to the last drop. I told you I'm not much of a drinker. Keith knew I couldn't possibly drink more than one margarita and think straight."

Jamy smirked. "If you weren't thinking straight, I'd bet it wasn't the margarita's fault." He scratched his head. "You know, Aleese, there was something Arman said…"

Aleese clutched Jamy's sleeve. "What?"

"Well, when I suggested there were other fish in the sea, he said, but not a woman like her." Jamy looked pleased with himself. "Wow, the power of Shiraz. It sure pricked my memory."

In the car, driving to the hotel with Jamy, Aleese was feeling a little buzzed. Did she know where Keith was? Did she care? No, but she'd have to take care of unfinished business…soon.

Jamy gave her a hug when they arrived at the Del Mar. "Look, honey. Keep in mind, Arman is wary of love. He had a tremendously bad experience with our girl Cisca." He sighed, "Poor Jack. He's always been a player, but he's involved with a master manipulator." He squeezed her hand. "Don't expect too much too fast from a man like Arman. Sex yes, love no."

And with those wise words, he zoomed off leaving her behind to ponder their meaning. It wasn't encouraging to know Arman might be back only to have some hot sex with her. Not that she minded hot sex, but it was the idea of being used and tossed away and then replaced by some other female. Aleese wanted a man to value her and appreciate her personality besides her physical attributes. She knew that might be a bit much to expect from a male, but she could dream.

She supposed they'd made a mistake from day one, approaching it backwards—the cart before the horse. Not a logical way to build a relationship with a man. She should have suppressed her physical desires and put her pussy on a back burner while she impressed Arman with her sense of humor and intelligence. But it was too late to play the innocent ingénue. He knew all too well how much she liked sex with him.

8

On her way to the elevator, Aleese wondered if Keith would be in their room. She didn't think so. He was an outgoing guy and if he'd hit it off with the tour group, in all likelihood, he would still be with them. As the elevator doors opened, Aleese glanced over at the bar, but didn't see him.

A heavy man and his wife went up to six and got off, leaving her to continue on up to the seventh floor. At the door, she dug in for her room key and was surprised to find the box of chocolates—ammunition in reserve. But those delicious morsels would have to wait for next time. A dark cloud spread doom on her usually optimistic outlook. Would there be a next time? She sighed. If she lost Arman, it would pierce a hole in her heart. She now realized how special he was. It was up to her to rectify the situation.

Resignedly, she opened the door. Once inside, she listened, but hearing no sounds from the bathroom, she realized she was alone. On the center of each newly-made bed, a swan made of towels sat. The maid was a romantic. She obviously didn't know this was the scene of impending disaster. Aleese had to admit she was more than a little nervous about attempting another talk with Keith. It might make more sense to text him first—prepare him. Taking her cell out of her bag, she tapped out a message.

We need to talk seriously. Meet me at the pool.

That should do it, she thought going over to the dresser to find a bathing suit. Keith always checked his messages, in case anything came in from work. As an engineer with Borish and Wilnot, a large automotive company, he was convinced they couldn't function without him.

The top drawer of the dresser had been claimed by Keith. She had the next two. Having organized her bathing suits together with her underwear, she quickly found a bikini and a coverup. Once she had the red and black string bikini tied, she padded over to the mirror to check herself out. Very nice, she thought, thinking how it was a shame to waste this outfit on Keith. Not that he'd notice. He probably thought her breasts were way too small after admiring the redhead's humongous knockers.

Seeing her image in the mirror ignited sizzling memories of the hallway where Arman had ignited a fire inside of her—a raging out of control forest fire. With Arman pressed against her, strong arms wrapped tightly, their reflections locked in a fiery embrace. Passionate kisses swept her into a river of hot molten lust—her body ready for his hard powerful thrusts. She grimaced. Just when she'd had the opportunity to win him over, Jamy and Jack had ruined it. Aleese could only hope he wanted to be with her as much as she longed to be with him. Slipping into her wedged sandals, Aleese gathered her strength, picked up her bag and headed out the door.

The trip down to the pool had her stomach twisted into knots. When she stepped into the bright sunlight, she heaved a sigh of relief—no Keith. She found an empty lounge chair and took it, settling down, her legs stretched out. The Shiraz had relaxed her and with the sun warming her body, Aleese drifted away into a place where dreams and memories mingled, Arman's arresting face surfacing before she was swept away into sleep.

A while later, Aleese awoke with a start—not sure how long she had been dozing. Remembering what she had to do, she sat up and surveyed the pool area. Keith must not have received her message, she thought anxiously, not spotting him. She was worried. Where was he?

Aleese took a few breaths to relax, but didn't quite succeed. Although a waiter was taking drink orders, he rushed by her chair and hurried on to a party of six. If she wanted a drink, she'd have to get one herself. Swinging her legs off the lounge chair, she stood up and headed to the pool bar.

The bartender, a square-faced young man, barely out of his teens, cocked his head to one side. "*Si, señorita*, what would you like?"

"A piña colada, please."

"Good choice. I make the best."

Aleese watched as he poured some coconut juice into a blender. When the bartender finished, he presented her with a substantial drink in an immense goblet decorated with a slice of pineapple. After trying it, Aleese glanced around the area for Keith with no luck. Nervously, she fiddled with her stir stick.

A German couple came up, ordered martinis and left. Swiveling around, she checked the tables for Keith and his tour group people, but he wasn't there.

Halfway through her drink, she heard the titters of a woman and a man's loud guffaws. Something was very familiar about the woman's laughter. Why? Suddenly it dawned on her. That irritating laugh belonged to the woman from the fort—the voluptuous redhead with the Indian skirt and revealing blouse. From the pool area, Keith and the redhead, along with a nondescript bespectacled man approached, each of them carrying an empty beer bottle.

"I see you're into the heavy stuff, Aleese," Keith commented snidely. "Hey, you two, this is Aleese." He waved his hand imperiously. "Jan and Ron. They did the fort tour with me yesterday."

"I gather you don't like forts," Ron said to Aleese while Keith spoke to the bartender about another round.

"Not at all. I rather enjoy history. I was anxious to see El Morro."

"But you didn't go?"

"Actually, I did," Aleese told Ron. "I took the earlier tour."

"Oh," Ron said puzzled, "I didn't know there was one." Leaning in closer to her, he whispered, "Have you and Keith had a fight?"

"Aleese tends to be moody," Keith interjected. "She was in a funk yesterday, so she and I decided to spend the day apart. Now Jan here knows what mellow is."

From under her floppy straw sunhat Jan smiled in a superior fashion. "What's not to be happy about?" she chirped.

While fixing on a smile, Aleese seethed inwardly. "Are you and Ron together?"

"Ron's my brother," Jan said. "Mom and Pappy thought we needed a family vacation." She waved her beer around. "We had such a lovely time yesterday. Too bad you weren't there, Alice. You should have seen Keith and Pappy—they were so funny."

Keith funny? That would have been something to see, Aleese thought dubiously.

"Those two made us all laugh so hard, we hardly heard the tour guide," Jan added.

"Too bad," Aleese said. "It was a great tour," she glared, "and my name is Aleese."

Jan giggled. "So sorry, Aleese. I'm so bad on names," she nudged Keith, "but good with other things."

Aleese rolled her eyes and grimaced. She turned to Keith. "We need to talk."

"And we can—later. Jan and Ron don't want to hear our problems, do you guys?"

"If it helps to talk, why not?" Jan sang out cheerfully.

Aleese was getting more and more annoyed by the woman. She sipped the last bit of her piña colada and waited for Keith to reply.

"Maybe you should speak with Jan, Aleese. She's a counselor at the hospital. That might be just what you need. Another woman to talk to," Keith said seriously.

"Me? You think I need help?" Aleese said in disbelief.

"You have been acting unexplainably bad-tempered lately."

"I was trying to tell you something, but you refused to listen," Aleese said tightly.

Ron took Jan's elbow and steered her away from the bar. "Come on, let's go."

Jan nodded. As they headed to the lobby, she called back to Keith, "We'll see you at dinner, okay?"

Keith smiled. "Sure thing." He turned to Aleese. That girl is loaded, would you believe? Her family owns a computer company but she still does that counselor job. Too kind for her own good. Now, you, on the other hand, could learn something from a woman like that." His lips turned down at the corners. "We're on vacation and it seems like there is one crisis after another with you, Aleese. It's getting tiresome." His eyes shot to Jan and Ron disappearing through the doorway.

"I think we need to get something straight."

"Oh?" Keith lifted an eyebrow and took a sip of his beer before he set it on the bar. "About what?"

"The two of us."

"If you are jealous of Jan, you needn't be. She's purely a friend."

"I'm not thinking about Jan. Last night, I tried to explain how I felt."

"You said you thought our goals differed."

"It's more than that, Keith. I think we aren't…"

"What?" Keith persisted.

"Well, I think we aren't compatible."

"This suddenly occurred to you?" Keith asked sarcastically.

With his tone so rude, Aleese gathered up her strengths and bravely voiced, "No, I've been thinking this for a while."

"To have a relationship it's not necessary to be identical twins. Haven't you heard the expression *vive la difference*?"

"Yes," Aleese sighed, "but we are too different."

"What are you suggesting?"

"I don't want to date you anymore."

Keith stared at her in disbelief. "I see," he said, before he turned on his heel and stalked out to the lobby.

Aleese watched him enter the lobby. She looked at the bartender who had set another piña colada in front of her.

"It's happy hour, *señorita*. Second one is free."

9

Aleese awoke, her head aching. She remembered finishing the second piña colada. Some guy had hit on her at the bar but she had managed to put him off and left for her room. In the elevator, she had noticed her bikini top was loose and dangerously close to sliding off. So that's why the jerk's eyes had been glued on her breasts, she thought angrily. Waiting for the free show, was he? Well, she'd foiled his plan. She bit her lip, thinking how close she'd been to making a fool of herself. It really hadn't been smart to down the second drink. It was all Keith's fault—arrogant bastard wouldn't face the truth. Her eyes shot over to the radio clock by her bed—7:10. Arman would be here soon. He must have landed by now.

Forcing herself to sit up, Aleese knew she'd have to hurry. On the bed beside her, she found her purse. Thoughtfully, she unzipped it and drew out the box of chocolates. They should have been taste tested earlier today, but with Arman angry, they'd never been opened. She hesitated a second before she took off the lid and eyed the truffles. Two rows of perfect chocolates delicately swirled with white icing. Unconsciously, Aleese took out a strawberry chocolate truffle from its pretty paper nest and held it between her two fingers.

The box was Arman's present. It wouldn't be right to eat one, but it looked so—irresistible. She brought it to her lips. She knew she shouldn't, but a powerful force came over her. The truffle flew in to the roof of her mouth where she held it in place, waiting for it to slowly melt. Ambrosia. Chocolate and strawberry flavors mingled magically, until finally, the last remnant of chocolate dissolved. The nectar of the gods lingered on her tongue and then coming to her senses, Aleese hastily slid the lid back on the box and shoved it tightly shut, disgusted with herself and her weakness. How could she have so little willpower? What kind of person would give a box of chocolates to a man she supposedly liked with one of them missing? She was disgusting.

Jumping off the bed, Aleese took herself from temptation and scurried into the bathroom. She needed to get ready for her date with Arman and it was essential she looked exceptionally alluring. Who knows what he had to say? She needed to be everything he desired in a woman.

In the shower she spread chocolate shower gel all over— specifically on her breasts, belly and pussy. Satisfied with her ministrations, she stepped out to dry herself and smoothed a chocolate scented lotion over every conceivable area of her body. She wanted to fill Arman's brain with endorphins—a release of these little suckers would have him panting for pleasure.

A few minutes later, her hair and makeup complete, Aleese fastened a lacy rose bra, and tugged on a pair of matching high-cut panties. This done, Aleese padded over to the closet to select a dress. On a hanger at the back, Aleese spied a silky pink dress. Never having worn it, she decided it was ready for a debut. She slipped it carefully over her head and straightened the straps before placing her feet in a pair of backless metallic sandals. Stepping back from the mirror, she admired her image. Perfect!

With a few minutes to spare, Aleese wandered over to the TV and turned it on. On the edge of the bed, ankles crossed, she tried to focus on the emergency hospital crisis. She had to wonder if Arman would even show up. He could have reconsidered and thought her situation with Keith was too bizarre for him. There'd be women with less complicated lives he could hook up with—like Shanna. Just as the patient's heart on screen flat-lined, there was a knock on the door and Aleese, her own heart racing, switched the TV off and clicked her way to the door.

Peering out of the peep hole, she was astonished to see a waiter with a room service cart. What was this all about? Hesitant to open the door, she undid it, leaving the chain in place.

The stocky waiter grinned widely. "*Buenos noches, señorita.*"

"I didn't order anything," Aleese told him. "This is a mistake."

"I hope not," Arman said stepping out. "I thought I'd surprise you."

"Oh-hh…" Aleese stood there a moment before she came to her senses and undid the chain. "Please, come in."

The waiter pushed in the cart with Arman following.

"Where would you like it?" the waiter asked.

"How about the balcony?" Arman suggested, looking at Aleese.

"Mm-mm," she said, still in shock. He was so gorgeous in his blue uniform, she was positively tongue-tied.

Unaware of her dilemma, Arman slid the doors open enabling the waiter to push the cart through. Outside, the sun had set, but a reddish glow streaked the clear dark blue sky. The ocean was wildly turbulent, waves crashing on the shore, lapping frothy white foam on the sandy beach.

The waiter stood to the side as Arman pulled out a chair for Aleese and one for himself, before he took a seat across from her. While the waiter lit the candles, Aleese gazed across the table at Arman, struck once again at how much she was attracted to him. In the candlelight, his sherry eyes glinted mysteriously. She wished she could read his mind.

The waiter systematically lifted the lid of each silver platter while explaining, "Mussels, crab legs, and for dessert..."

Arman interrupted, "*Gracias,* but we would like the wine, *por favor.*"

"*Perdonneme, señor,*" the waiter said quickly and inserted a corkscrew into a bottle of deep-scarlet wine, pulling out the cork. Pouring a dribble into one glass, he gave it to Arman, who swirled the wine before he brought it to his lips. When he nodded approvingly, the waiter filled their glasses.

Sipping the maroon liquid, Aleese asked, "Shiraz?"

"Yes, you do have a discerning palate," he said, handing the waiter a tip. After the server headed out the door, Arman gazed at Aleese. "Do you like it?"

"Very much," she said thinking how delicious he looked.

He lifted up a lid. "Steamed mussels?"

"Yes, please."

Arman dug one out and brought it to her mouth. She parted her lips and let him deposit the mussel. A morsel that left her wanting more. She wasn't disappointed when he dug up another for her to savor. It was an unusual experience. Being fed by a succulent man was something that had never happened to her before.

After the third mussel, Aleese wanted to feel less like a bystander. She took up her fork and scooped up a mussel. "Open," she said softly to Arman.

When he parted his sensuous lips, it was all Aleese could do not to toss the mussel away and kiss him passionately, but she didn't.

He had arranged this romantic dinner and for years, she had been looking for a sensitive man and now that she'd found one, she wouldn't let passion spoil it. She would enjoy the romantic dinner before she pounced on him, unless of course he didn't want her anymore. Examining his face for any evidence of this, Aleese came up with nothing. Arman was far from being an open book.

He allowed her to feed him one more mussel before he waved his hand and said, "No, you need to eat, Aleese. I can see how hungry you are."

And she was—for him. Had he suggested going to his place for a sample, Aleese would have put her stomach on hold. But as she glanced through the glass into her empty hotel room, she was not keen on starting her exploration here.

"I hope you like crab legs?" Arman grabbed the tongs and placed one on her plate.

"I do—very much." Dipping the meat into the heated butter, Aleese forced herself to broach the subject on her mind. "Arman?"

"Yes?"

"Did you have a good trip?"

Arman's mouth turned up slightly at the corners. "It was fine, but rather inopportune."

"You mean because…"

"We have a lot to talk about, don't we, Aleese?" Arman's eyes searched her face. "What's the situation with your boyfriend?"

She gazed at him from over the rim of her glass. "My ex."

"You told him?"

Aleese nodded.

"And does he understand?"

Aleese sighed and forked up some crab. "I hope so."

Arman drank his wine contemplatively. "Where is he?"

"Went out with his friends in the tour group."

"So we have the place to ourselves for the evening?"

Aleese nodded, meeting his eyes. His stare was so intense, she felt heat rise to her cheeks.

Arman reached across the table and took up her hand. "It's so small and delicate—like you." Turning her hand, he kissed her wrist.

A current jolted her body.

"I thought about you on the plane."

"Good thoughts?"

His eyes glimmered. "Purely wicked ones."

"Does that mean," Aleese said hesitantly, "I've been forgiven?"

"It's not that simple." He placed his hand on the last platter and took the lid off. "Dessert?"

"Oh-hh, my…" Aleese's mouth watered at the sight of the chocolate mousse cake.

"I know you were disappointed with the coconut dessert, so I thought I'd get you some chocolate," Arman smiled suggestively, "to wake up those endorphins."

"Mm-mm. You're right about that. I feel a pleasurable rush every time I eat chocolate."

Arman laid a slice on her plate and one for himself. He watched her as she sampled the cake.

"Orgasmic!"

"I'll need to work hard to beat that then."

Heat rose to Aleese's cheeks. Her thoughts raced to the fort and then to the interrupted moments in the hallway. It had all been hot beyond belief, but did he really want to make love? Who was she kidding—it was sex and of course he wanted it. What man didn't? And then, to be honest herself, what passionate woman wouldn't?

To hide her confusion, she ate more cake. When she had consumed every last savory bit, she glanced up to see, Arman staring at her. Had she been too enthusiastic in her cake consumption or was it something else? She lifted her glass and sipped her wine wondering if she should broach the subject of his feelings for her. Would it scare him if she did?

Collecting her thoughts, she got up and leaned on the balcony. The breeze swirled her dress, lifting it up. Holding the unruly skirt down, Aleese watched the heavy mass of dark clouds moving in. "I think we're in for a storm."

From behind her, Arman said, "Put your glass down."

Startled by the request, Aleese did as he asked. Swinging her around, his lips replaced the glass and the soft bouquet of the wine became the warmth of his mouth. Tenderly, he teased her— sucking each lip, until her rapid breathing was replaced by sighs.

When his tongue entered her waiting mouth Aleese was on fire. Her eager fingers ran over the curve of his ass, squeezing possessively, as she pressed him close. Against the heat of her body, his rod stirred restlessly.

Arman dropped down to kneel in front of her. She was his altar to worship. Lightly skimming her legs, he stoked her flames like no man had ever done before. Aleese felt captured. Arman was devastatingly handsome in the navy blue uniform. Mesmerized by the dark curls spilling over his collar, tingles coursed to her core. The velvety tip of Arman's tongue flicked on the tender skin at back of her knee and upwards to her soft inner thigh. Like a drowning victim on a sinking ship she gripped the railing tightly—white knuckling with each journeying kiss.

A saucy sea breeze tousled her hair, leaving a salty film on her skin, heightening her awareness. Arman pressed her thighs, for a glimpse of her pink treasure. Threading fingers through the coal-black curls, she was transported into another realm, yet distantly, from far below, she heard the voices of evening partiers. Latin music from the bar band floated up. Unconsciously, Aleese brought a hand up to stroke her breast, fingertips searching under the flimsy fabric for her hardened nipple.

Impatiently, Arman jerked her panties to her ankles. She met his eyes—smoldering with arousal. Lifting her foot, Aleese kicked the lacy garment away. A gust of wind blew her dress up to her waist. Cool breeze fanned her steamy skin. Shivering more from anticipation than from the chill, Aleese closed her eyes, heightening her senses. Each flick of Arman's tongue fired a flame. As if in answer to her silent prayer, Arman's curled fingers entered her soaking slit. Aleese pushed her pelvis forward as the wind unleashed the rain.

Throwing the lounge cushions on the cement, Arman urged, "Lay down."

Aleese lowered herself to the ground, her back resting on the pillows as drops splattered on her face and arms. Above her, Arman shielded Aleese from the pelting rain, greeting her waiting lips with a bruising kiss that drew her in like iron filings to a magnet.

Fiercely, Aleese gripped a lock of thick hair as hot kisses burned her body. Lost in lust, she threw her head back, exposing her throat—vulnerable to the rain and to Arman. Heatedly, her lover attacked the defenseless hollow. Aleese went limp, willing him to take her. But Arman wanted to make her climb higher on passion's summit. He had never wanted a woman more. The soft and silky skin of her breast was irresistible—her nipple ripe for his lips. Drawing it in and releasing it in slow motion, he groaned like a beast in agony—because he was. She was the goddess he needed as much as life itself.

Aleese floated on an ethereal cloud—where no one else existed except Arman. The rain's cold fingers assaulted her, heightening the intensity of her senses. Aleese pushed Arman to her breast and held him tightly as her pleasure mounted. Electric current from the tips of his long fingers shot to the contours of her body— every nerve ending awakened. Aleese floated in a cloud of euphoria, never wanting to return.

But the storm came in with a vengeance, soaking them to the skin. Arman carried a shivering Aleese inside and gently laid her down on the bed. Water dripped off his forehead. Time stopped. Slowly, Aleese stroked his cheek until Arman caught up her fingers and sucked each digit in turn, his dark eyes glittering like amber.

A clatter from the hall door startled them. Keith stepped in. His clothes were dry, untouched by the storm. "Aleese," he said slowly, staring in confusion, taking in the wet hair and clothing. "What's going on?"

"Keith, this is my friend." Aleese explained hesitantly.

Taking the initiative, Arman stood up and strode over, extending his hand. "Arman. We were caught in the rain," he said in way of explanation.

"Of course," Keith said automatically, shaking Arman's hand. "There's quite a storm out there." He eyed Arman's uniform. "You're a pilot?"

Arman shook his head. "No, a flight attendant—American Airlines."

"I'm sure it's an interesting job," Keith said somewhat condescendingly.

"It can be," Arman said smiling. "Aleese tells me you are an engineer."

Keith nodded enthusiastically. "For three years now. It's challenging, but I enjoy it." He looked at Arman curiously. "You must have seen a few places."

"Asia, Europe, South America and a few routes in the US. I was lucky enough to travel on other airlines we work with. Do you like to travel?"

Keith frowned. "This trip is my first outside of Montreal. I'm from Toronto. You?"

"New York originally, but I've lived in a few different places."

"American, are you?"

"Dual citizenship—Canadian and American." Arman glanced at Aleese's wet dress. "You might want to change. Take some things with you."

Aleese nodded, avoiding Keith's questioning look. There was no way she'd tell him the plan. In fact, she didn't know what the plan was or what she'd be doing tonight, but she wanted to be prepared.

Keith grimaced watching Aleese fill her carry-on bag with an assortment of items from the dresser. What the hell was she thinking taking off with a flight attendant? For God's sake, they'd been talking marriage and Aleese thought she could just walk out on him*? He'd come back early from dinner so they could straighten things out between them and now she was leaving?* "Where are you going, Aleese?" Keith asked sharply.

Aleese swung around and stared at him. "Out." She turned to Arman. "I'm ready."

"You need to think this over, Aleese. You're making a big mistake. He's nothing but a player. Surely you can see that?"

Arman's intense eyes challenged Keith. "Aleese is an adult, fully capable of making her own decisions." He gripped the bag and opened the door and waited.

Keith shot Arman a disdainful glance before he commented, "You'll regret this, Aleese." When she didn't answer him, he called out after them, "I won't be so kind when you come crawling back!"

10

At the front of the hotel, Arman hailed a cab. The driver pulled up under the awning. "*Buenos noches*. Where to?"

Arman said something rapidly in Spanish and helped Aleese in. "Are you okay, sweetheart?" he asked, looking at Aleese rubbing her forehead.

"A headache. Just stress."

Pulling her close, Arman massaged the back of her neck and shoulders. "You handled it fine. Relax. It's all over."

"I'll try." She didn't know if she should ask him about staying at his place. She had assumed he wanted her to stay overnight when he'd asked her to pack some things, unless, she thought, staring sadly at her damp dress, he was thinking she looked like something the cat dragged in and simply wanted her to change.

"You're not afraid of him, are you?"

Aleese's eyes widened. "You think he might get violent?"

"I don't know him." Arman stroked her cheek with his finger. "If there's any possibility of..."

The driver interrupted, "*Señor*, where do I turn?"

"See the bakery? Turn right there."

The man grunted in reply.

"Slow down. It's the one with the black fence." Arman pointed to the white stucco house with the bougainvillea tree. "There."

When the cab came to a halt, Arman reached over and handed the driver some bills and then grabbing the bag, helped Aleese out. A few lights on in the house. They would not be alone in the hallway this time.

"Looks like someone's home," Arman said glancing at the movement behind the blind in the kitchen. Why don't we go to my room?" he said, as they entered.

Aleese dug in her purse and brought up the box of chocolates. "These are for you, Arman. I meant to give them to you earlier, but..."

Arman grinned. "I think you already gave me a treat that I really appreciated, Aleese, but," he said glancing at the box in his hands,

"I'm sure the chocolate will be almost as delicious." He stooped down and kissed her lips slowly. "Why don't we go try some?"

Placing his hand at the small of her back, he steered her down the hall to a room with a large oak door. Aleese recognized it from before. The room was sizable with large double windows, a desk in the corner, an enormous armoire and a four-poster king-sized bed. When he flicked on the lights, the bedside lamps cast a golden glow on the wood furnishings.

Aleese watched as Arman took the lid off and placed it at the bedside table. "Nice choice." He grinned. "I suppose the milk chocolates are for you?"

"I took the liberty of testing one to make sure they were edible. Hope you don't mind?"

"Then it's my turn."

In a throaty voice, Aleese agreed. "Yes, Arman. It is…"

Large fluffy pillows and tan sheets. Clean and inviting, Aleese thought, except for the strange lump in the middle. Had he covered a pillow when he had made his bed? The last time she'd been there, Arman had been packing and dressing for his flight while she had been hastily locating her clothing.

When the sheets started to move, Aleese froze. The lumpy pillow transformed into a lovely brunette, appearing from under the covers. "Arman," she said slowly, taking in their soggy appearances, "ahm so sorry. Ah thought y'd be by yer lonesome."

"Shanna," Arman said quickly, "what are you doing here?"

Aleese was stunned. She couldn't get her eyes off the brunette who was now sitting up, the sheet barely hiding her breasts. Aleese turned to Arman and stared. The man before her was a stranger. Her fabulous lover was a cheater having a clandestine affair with another woman. The bastard thought he could hide it from her before she left for Toronto.

"Ah had no idea. Ya never told me 'bout yuh two."

"That's because there was nothing to tell, was there, Arman?" Aleese picked up her bag and bee-lined to the door. "We are not involved."

"Well that's just wunnerful. Ah'd hate to be interruptin' anythang. Hey, sugah, look at this pretteh lil' scarf ah found." She pulled up a yellow print scarf from under the covers and waved it in the air for them to see.

"Wait, Aleese," Arman called after her, "don't go. Shanna and I aren't..."

Aleese swung around and glared at him. "How stupid do you think I am? You've been sleeping with her. Why else would she be waiting for you in your bed?"

"Tell her," Arman said, glaring at his crew member. "Have we ever had sex?"

"Na," Shanna said hesitantly.

"Get dressed," Arman said tightly.

Aleese's eyes registered on the yellow scarf in Shanna's hand. "That's my scarf!" Striding up to the bed, she snatched it out of Shanna's hand.

"Let's give her some privacy," Arman said to Aleese hastily. Taking her elbow, he led her out into the hall.

"She can have all the privacy she needs and so can you!" Aleese jerked her arm away.

"Aleese, sweetheart, listen to her. I had nothing..."

"I heard. She had to say that. You're her boss. She wouldn't want to rub you the wrong way."

Tinkling laughter. Cisca stepped into the hallway. "So right you are, Aleese. Shanna *would* want to rub our naughty boy the right way."

Arman's eyes narrowed. "What do you know about all this, Cisca?"

"Me?"

Arman closed in on her. "Yes, you!"

Cisca backed up to the wall.

"Did you tell Shanna to wait in my bedroom?"

"No, sugah, don' git angry wit her," Shanna said smoothly from behind. "Ah didn't know yuh was goin' with anyone when ah came ovah. It was all mah idea. Thought you might like some comp'ny."

Cisca snickered. "I merely showed her where to wait. I had no idea anyone was with you." She turned to Aleese. "Just a little joke on all of us, *amiga*. Don't take it so seriously. Come into the kitchen, Shanna. I'll make us a snack."

Shanna, looking smart in her blue uniform, smiled broadly at Cisca, "Shuh thang. We ain't had no girl talk fuh ages." She sashayed into the kitchen, followed by Cisca.

On the point of tears, Aleese swung around and rushed to the door.

"Don't forget your bag, Aleese," Cisca called out from the kitchen.

Embarrassed besides feeling betrayed and angry, Aleese returned to get her bag. Clasping the bag in one hand and the scarf in the other, she raced to the front door, fumbled with the handle and pulled it ajar.

Arman pushed the door back. "We need to talk." There was no way he was letting her leave.

"I'm going," Aleese insisted. "This conversation is over!"

Arman gave her a look before he swung her up into his arms and carried her to his room. If she didn't realize how important she was to him, he'd have to show her.

"Stop, put me down! I mean it, Arman. I'm not staying here with you."

Ignoring her protests, Arman kicked the door shut, brought her over to the bed and dropped her down. Tossing her bag on the floor, he slipped the silk scarf from her hand around her wrist.

Aleese sat up. "Let me go! We're over. Do you hear?"

Arman straddled her, his eyes intense. "Calm down, Aleese. It was all Cisca's doing. You should know what she's capable of." His mouth turned up suddenly at the corners, with his sudden insight. "But maybe, you just wanted to be captured."

"What?"

Arman had the feeling Aleese needed some proof that he wanted her, not Shanna. And she was a strong-willed stubborn woman. Quickly he brought her wrists together, loosely wrapping the scarf around them before he looped the end into a knot.

Aleese stared at him, her big blue eyes wide.

"What are you doing, Arman?" she asked uncertainly.

Surely, she didn't think he'd hurt her. "Aleese, I want you to listen to me."

"Let me go and I'll promise to listen."

Arman glanced at her lovely face, doubting her words. She was lying, trying to appease him, he thought. He had to try to change her mind. Bringing the edge of her skirt up, he slid his hand over her thigh. Her skin was velvety smooth and her leg felt so firm, Arman's cock grew instantly stiff and swollen. As his hand stroked her inner thigh, he heard Aleese sigh involuntarily.

Resting his elbow on the bed, he leaned in to kiss her pouty mouth—lips that cried out for him. "You're so beautiful, Aleese," he whispered huskily before he pressed his lips on hers, in a demanding kiss that she allowed passively. All that they had wouldn't end now. Not if he could help it. He caressed her mouth—first the upper and then the lower lip before he thrust the tip of his tongue between. It was like sweet music filling his very being.

When Aleese sank back into the pillow and gazed up at him he wondered what thoughts were racing through her head. He'd almost lost her. He wouldn't let that happen. Watching her arch her back, breasts thrust forward, was very hot. *Could this be her way of showing her need for him—like a lioness does to her mate?* He hoped it was because now he had an overwhelming urge to touch her everywhere—explore every part of her body until she begged for him to fuck her. But first, he needed to convince Aleese that he was genuine.

The lovely curve of her neck beckoned him. He felt her respond with a tremor as he licked his way to the hollow of her throat while his hand slid the strap of her dress down her arm. He sucked the smooth skin of her shoulder again and again until she shuddered. Tantalizing her further with more licks, Aleese's ragged breathing gave him his answer.

He found a zipper at the side of her dress and pulled it with one hand while his lips journeyed to her enticing breasts. When he tugged the fabric down to her waist, he discovered the strapless lacy bra that covered them—gift wrapping for a much desired present.

"Arman, no, stop this! I'm not your plaything," she protested, squirming away. "Go find one of your other women."

"There's no need to find any woman, besides you. What we have between us is magic. You're not my toy. Aleese, believe me—no other woman has ever done this to me before." Turning her to him, he unfastened the hooks and slid the lacy garment off. He hesitated, searching her face to see if she understood. Wasn't she feeling that electricity between them? Didn't she want him to continue his voyage to unleash her passion?

Arman sighed. She must be in denial. The proof was in her

body's reaction. Hadn't she just wriggled as he kissed his way to those magnificent mounds? Or was this all wishful thinking on his part? Aleese was resisting him and seeing the flush of anger on her face, he knew it would be an uphill battle. Arman smiled. He was up for the challenge.

His eyes feasted on her taut peaks. He stroked them, fingering her nipples lightly. She will want to be mine, he thought confidently. Folding her breasts closer together, he licked the hollow between. With each lick, her chest rose and fell more quickly. I will make her want me, Arman vowed.

He throbbed to enter her tight hot pussy and if his dick could speak he would be asking him to hurry. Arman smiled, thinking the big guy was being very patient considering he had been denied often enough. But, Aleese needed time. His needs would have to wait.

"Chocolate?"

"Mm-mm," Aleese murmured with a faint smile, her eyes lighting up.

Taking one from the box, he placed it between his teeth and brought his mouth up to her lips.

With her lids half-closed, she bit off a morsel of the truffle, and savored the candy. While she was thus occupied, Arman ate his and slid her dress down to her hips. Once she had swallowed the chocolate, he pushed her onto her back.

"My turn," he said softly, taking a dark chocolate and setting it on her nipple. He glanced up at Aleese. Her lips had parted and her turquoise eyes glittered with what he hoped was excitement. If it wasn't, he'd make sure she enjoyed the truffle as much as he. The chocolate was delicious, but nothing compared to the pleasure of drawing her nipple into his mouth and sucking the erect tip. While he nibbled on one mound, his hand played with her other breast, kneading her nipple. Aleese squirmed under him, her breathing irregular and when he heard a low moan, he knew she was ready to surrender.

Taking a chance that he was right, Arman sat up, hastily unbuttoned his jacket and jerked it off. He checked to see if Aleese had her guard up, but she laid passively watching, eyes focused on his chest. Quickly, he tore off his shirt, throwing it on the floor where it joined the jacket. In a flash, he unbuckled his pants and opened the zipper, gazing at Aleese. Her eyes centered on his ram-rod hard tool straining to break out of his boxer-briefs.

He couldn't take his eyes off of her. Lying nearly nude on his bed, Aleese was a goddess. Pear-shaped mounds tipped with rosy nipples, a narrow waist and shapely legs—metallic stilettos adorning her dainty feet. Her frothy lilac dress was bunched up around her waist, a piece of the skirt draping down to cover her pussy. Her treasure—soon to be his.

From his bedside table he pulled out a small curved object and a bottle.

"What's that?" Her voice had an edge.

"I want you to experience the joy of being my captive." After he squirted a few drops of liquid from a bottle, onto the silicone toy, he set it on a tissue. "It'll all be for your pleasure," he said, gently pushing up her dress. No panties. Ah, yes, he'd forgotten. From the balcony earlier, the precious lacy item was securely tucked in his pocket.

Arman bent down. Aleese let him access her pussy without protest. His tongue greedily licked her folds searching for her clit. He inhaled her scent—spicy, yet sweet...intoxicating. Finding the pink bud, he cupped the cheeks of her nicely-rounded ass to bring her closer to him. Lightly flicking, he persisted until she wiggled away. He was forced to take a tighter hold to ensure her bud got all his attention, but Aleese made him work for her treasure. The more he feathered her clit, the more she fought it, squeezing her thighs against the sides of his head. His ears were sore with the pressure. Finally, he lost contact with her swollen clit. Was she refusing him, trying to keep him away? Puzzled, Arman brought his head up and glanced up at Aleese.

"Don't stop, Arman!" she whispered urgently. "I feel so close."

He spread her thighs gently as he would open the petals on a delicate flower. Keeping his hands on her inner thighs, he said softly, "Leave them open, sweetheart. It's the only way. I want to give your clit what it needs, but your thighs are making it a bit uncomfortable."

"Oh-hh," Aleese breathed in an effort to explain, spreading her legs again, while Arman resumed his licking, "it's just that I like to come with my legs together. The tension makes..." she paused, losing her drift.

Rhythmically flicking her sensitive core, Arman slid his tongue down and licked up her nectar, his lust heightening with every lap.

Her juices tasted like a mixture of morning dew and dark chocolate. He wanted to drink up every drop of her juice. His mouth covered her silky folds and he sucked them before he allowed his fingers to explore her soaking slit. He curled them into her pussy to press against her inner pleasure spot. In and out—over and over, until Aleese let out a low moan.

By her writhing, Arman sensed she was coming close to orgasm. Her pussy needed more attention, he thought. He dipped his tongue into her succulent juices, before he traced the soft folds. Finally back on her clit, he licked harder than ever. Her pelvis shoved into his upper lip, but, he stuck to her like glue.

Aleese's scream was music to his ears, but he knew better than to stop. No. She needed more to make it last. Her pelvis jerked against him vigorously, but Arman knew her orgasm was just beginning and he'd make her come like she'd never come before. The tip of his tongue went crazy—flicking with lightening speed. He held her legs down as she lost control, a scream tearing out of her. Violently trembling, Aleese let out a low moan and jerked again and moaned once more before her legs went limp.

Shoving his briefs off, Arman picked up the toy and coated it with lube before he slipped it on his finger. Between her legs, he was rock-hard and ready. Arman glanced down. His swollen tool wanted her badly, but Arman had no intention of giving in. Aleese pulled her legs up and looked at him expectantly. Arman smiled slowly. Collecting her thighs, he pushed a pillow under her ass and let his dick nudge her folds.

"Arman…"

"Yes?"

"I want you," Aleese said breathlessly, in a smoky voice.

Arman inserted his cock ever so slightly and heard her sigh. He willed it not to move.

"Arman…" she purred.

"Yes, babe?"

"Why aren't you…?"

"Why aren't I fucking you?"

"Yes."

Playing this game was taking every ounce of will power Arman possessed. "Do you believe me now?"

"Yes, I do—please do me!" Aleese pleaded.

Quickly pulling on the finger vibe, Arman remembered to bring his toy to her tender folds before he plunged hard into Aleese's waiting pussy. When her inner muscles gripped his stiff member he had to fight to stay in control. He wanted to come so badly, yet he held himself back.

When Aleese brought her legs up higher and rested them on his shoulders, his rod was in heaven. Ramming into her tight pussy, Arman rode joyously into a wet dream.

* * * *

Fucking had never made Aleese come. Not that it didn't make her feel good. When she'd already had an orgasm, it added another dimension. She'd always allowed it to go on and enjoyed the sensation until the repeated motion and position bored her. Then she'd coax her boyfriend to finish by squeezing her pelvic muscles. But this time it was different. Arman had a sizeable, thick tool that wouldn't let off. He filled her powerfully and with the addition of that little pulsing toy of his, Arman had succeeded in setting her throbbing clit into spasms. She would have been happy just to lie back and experience an exceptional fuck, but apparently, Arman had another plan.

Aleese felt herself fall down on her side, face to face with Arman, her bound hands pressed against him—helpless, yet, enveloped lovingly in his energy. His sensuous lips came to her in a deep driving kiss, setting her off the planet while each sizzling thrust of his rigid rod was returned with another of her own. She closed her eyes and touched his firm muscular chest. A sheen of moist sweat coated his skin. His clean soapy smell filled her senses—floating into bliss. No drug could be sweeter.

The vibes from the finger toy against her throbbing core, combined with Arman's stiff weapon, pushed her down a hot molten river. Time faded. The pleasure grew so intense it mingled with pain. Her moans charged the air. Each breath she took merged with his. She wanted it to go on forever, but her body cried out for release.

Arman's large hand cupped her from behind while his lubed fingertips slid into the tight opening of her ass. Keith had never done this and at first she didn't know if she liked the invasion, but with his finger slippery, it aroused her primal senses. Now, every part of her was tuned to him. Lips and tongues in a torrid tribal dance while she rocked with the driving force of his rod hitting her G-spot.

Aleese screamed, her body fiercely shaking in the first throngs of orgasm. In a last effort to make him come with her, she gave him a pelvic squeeze before she was hurled over the edge. Moaning, Aleese dropped her head onto his shoulder and pierced his skin with her teeth. Euphoric with pleasure—she shuddered, consumed by her orgasm, which didn't quit. With the momentum of his thrusting cock, Aleese lost control. Trembling, she dug her fingernails into his chest. Arman let out a low growl, worthy of a tiger and jerked. Hot liquid filled her. With one last jolt the rest of his cum spurted out. Their steamy bodies collapsed against each other.

11

Five months later

Fire-engine red toenails—with a shimmer. Perfect in or out of her red patent-leather stilettos, Aleese thought. Any minute now, Arman would have a thrill he wouldn't soon forget. She remembered his e-mail in reply to her suggestion.

Dear lovely Aleese: Change is good. You know me. Bring it on.
xxxxxxxxxxxxxxxxA

Had Arman really meant it? Aleese glanced down at her sandals. They were exceptionally high, and she mused, extremely sexy. One look at these and he'd forget about all the airline business and be ready for her fantasy flight. It would be a way to celebrate his return to his new job. His seven week course had taken far too much time—time they could have used productively together. E-mails and phone calls no matter how romantic were no substitute for the real thing. Now that he was back in Toronto, she wanted to see him as much as possible.

Thinking of the last few months of her life, Aleese pursed her lips. She must have been demented to have considered Keith as a future husband and father. All along she'd been right about Arman's intelligence and ambition.

If she was with the stodgy engineer, she wouldn't be sitting here in this flimsy outfit. A homecoming would have meant her cooking dinner for Keith—steak, well-done. In a conservative dress covered by an apron, she'd be waiting on him, hand and foot. Keith was high maintenance—lots of work with little appreciation shown in return. On the other hand, she smiled wickedly—Arman was much easier to please. For her bad boy, dinner would be secondary, unless she was the dessert.

Aleese glanced around the room to see if everything was in place. Satisfied that everything was just as it should be, she headed out to the lounge. *Enamorado Por Primera Vez*—in love for the first time, played softly. It was the perfect ambiance. Enrique's voice made her tingle for her Spanish man. There was something to be said for a Latin lover.

A knock on the door startled her. It had to be Arman. Now that the moment had arrived, her stomach somersaulted like an upside down rollercoaster ride. Would she be able to pull it off? Glancing down at the short black robe, she tightened the sash before she pulled the door open.

Leaning his back against the door frame, Arman gazed at Aleese—his mercurial dark eyes dancing with excitement as they swept down her body. Seeing him made her pulse race. His asymmetrical face was a powder keg of sexuality. Her hands begged to glide down his long lean frame, over his narrow waist and down to the firm curve of his ass, but she stopped herself. She needed to play a cool game in order to pull off this fantasy.

His bourbon eyes scorched her skin. "Aleese, you're even more beautiful than I remembered."

"And you are devastatingly handsome." Aleese took in his muscular body in the blue American Airlines uniform and sighed. "Do you think they might let you wear your uniform once you're working at the airport?"

"Only if I'm teaching a course." He grinned wickedly. "But nothing's stopping me from wearing it just for you, baby." Arman clicked the door shut behind him and set his bag on the floor.

"Mm-mm," Aleese murmured, conjuring up a sexy image of him. Now, she was even more anxious to start. Arman had said he would enjoy it, but still, it was a risk. He was a very masculine male and this was not typical.

Apparently, Arman was not feeling any stress about her undisclosed idea. Pulling her close, he brought his full lips to hers in a deep kiss. His tongue sparked her mouth with a lick that fired her core. She returned his thrust with one of her own and felt his heat enter her body.

It took a superwoman effort on Aleese's part to stop herself from throwing him down on the hardwood and kissing every part of him. Gathering her resolve, she suggested, "Why don't we sit first," gesturing to the red velveteen love seat.

"First," Arman questioned, a glimmer in his intense dark eyes, "before we..."

Aleese felt her cheeks flush and hastened to explain, "It's been so long since we've been together. I thought we might have some wine." On the coffee table she had set two crystal glasses and an open bottle of red. "I've let the Shiraz breathe, but it should be ready by now."

Taking the initiative, Arman picked up the bottle and poured them each a glass. "I'm curious about your fantasy."

"If you'd rather not..."

He smiled. "I meant every word that I wrote." Arman picked up his glass and toasted, "*Salud.*"

"I'm glad," Aleese said, clicking his glass. "To..."

"Us," Arman finished. I have a little present for you."

"Really? How sweet, Arman. But why?"

"Remember when I first saw you in the café in San Juan? You were eating a chocolate croissant?"

Aleese wasn't likely to forget that moment. In a white shirt and jeans, Arman had sizzled with a heat most men would envy. "Yes, you came in and ordered coffee," she said softly, excited by the memory.

"This is the five month anniversary of that day."

"It is?" Aleese's eyes lit up when she saw the tiny package wrapped in gold cellophane paper. "Now I feel bad. I have nothing to give you."

"I don't need anything, goddess." His eyes roamed down her short black silk robe and rested on her legs a moment before he studied her face. "Only you."

"Should I open it?"

Arman nodded, sat back in the couch and watched her tackle the ribbon.

Tugging on one end, the ribbon loosened and Aleese was able to undo it. Through the clear gold wrapping, she could see a jar. Removing the crinkly cellophane, she saw a dark brown jar with a metallic lid. Curious about the contents, Aleese twisted the bottle around and read the gold lettering. "Body chocolate?"

"Yes," Arman said his mouth turning up at the corners. "I thought we could try some tonight."

Not one to back down from chocolate at any time, Aleese grinned. "I'm sure we can accommodate it somehow. "Wait here," she said, taking the jar and disappearing into the bedroom to place it on the end table. She was about to rush back to Arman, but the temptation was too great. The top made a satisfying pop as she twisted the lid off. Sticking one finger into the dark swirl, she brought a drop of chocolate to her lips. The amazing chocolate syrup set her endorphins jumping. Not satisfied with one dip, she brought her finger back into the jar and sampled it once again. Then leaving the lid off, she waltzed back into the living room and sat down.

"Was it good?" Arman asked.

"How did you…"

Arman leaned over and very lightly skimmed her lips with the tip of his tongue. "Tasty…" he said giving her a lusty look.

"Mm-mm." Determined to stick to her plan, Aleese leaned back against the couch and sipped her wine. If he started licking her now, that would be the end of her plan. And there was something else she needed to find out.

Aleese regarded Arman solemnly. She had to know if things were still the same between them. When she'd first come back to Toronto, Arman had transferred here. They'd offered him a management position with an opportunity for advancement.

For the last few months, all had been well in their relationship. But now, with Arman away teaching the flight attendant's course, she had questions. It was the right time to have the talk—to dig into what was in his mind and his heart. "How did the course go?"

"An interesting change for me. I liked it, but I suppose you should be asking the students."

"I'm sure the women loved you," Aleese said, envisioning a nightmare of fifty Shannas popping out of his bed. "All of them learning the art of being the perfect flight attendant from my very charming boyfriend."

Arman laughed. "Not all. Some of them have regular jobs, like sales and banking. It surprised them what the job really entailed. The rose-colored glasses flew off and some of them quit." He grinned. "There were quite a few males, too, by the way, sweetheart, and many matronly females, mothers and grandmothers."

"I'm sure there had to have been some perky young things."

Arman smiled slowly. His eyes swept from her lovely face, to her full breasts, lower to her narrow waist, over the curve of her hips and down her shapely legs, all the way to her feet in the red stilettos. "Believe me, baby, no other woman could possibly have your allure. You are a goddess—the others, merely mortals." He drank his wine and glancing over at her added, "I regret I had to leave you for most of the summer. It would have been wonderful to have spent it with you on the beach." He paused. His changeable eyes locked with hers. "You haven't been seeing someone else, have you?"

Aleese brought her foot alongside his leg and slid it up and down, gazing into his eyes. "And if I had?" she teased.

"I'd have to use all my powers of persuasion to assure you that I'm more exciting than your latest conquest."

Aleese frowned. "So it wouldn't bother you if I'd found another boyfriend?" It was useless for her to deny that she was in love with him. Her heart beat faster whenever she opened his e-mails, but if he didn't have deep feelings for her...

"I wouldn't be upset if he were another engineer-type because you would know inwardly that he could never fulfill you in the way I could. You'd see that in a matter of days and break up with him."

That was true. She had come to realize that Keith had never understood her. Perhaps his overly logically mind couldn't connect with her creative side or she had given in to him once too often. He always wanted control and gave her no opportunity to express herself, nor did he value her opinions or thoughts. She glanced back at Arman and probed, "And if he was a pilot?" Arman knew how she was attracted to men in uniforms and pilots were one notch above flight attendants in the sexual sizzle scale.

"That would be a challenge." He ran a finger down her cheek. "But remember, they are men with sizeable egos and on the practical side," he added, "a pilot wouldn't be here in Toronto long enough to satisfy your cravings. And I know you'd worry about the layovers on the other end."

"So you'd be the better choice?"

"Now that I'm working at Pearson International, I'm at your disposal. Sure, once in a while, I'll be teaching the flight course, but I'm hoping you might go with me next time. How does a few weeks in New York sound to you?"

"It wouldn't be easy to get the time off. Teaching doesn't allow it," she said thoughtfully, "but I might request a short term leave." Was he just going through the motions, or did he really want her to go with him? If she couldn't join him anyway, he wouldn't have to feel guilty. He could take off and have fun without her. If he found a woman there, she'd be none the wiser.

"I could see if they have a summer course," Arman suggested, "and ask to teach it. How would that be? We could fly out to the Bahamas on the weekends. Coral reefs. Do you think you're up to doing some diving or snorkeling? Oh, and something else—some of the islands are uninhabited."

"That would be so-oo..." Aleese had a picture of them on an isolated beach entwined in an embrace.

Arman's whiskey eyes glinted. "Romantic—a place for lovers."

"Ah-hh. You read my mind." How different he was from any man she'd ever met—romantic, sensual and spontaneous. It dawned on Aleese that she didn't want to be without him nor did she want to be just a casual girlfriend. Somehow, tonight, she had to find out what their relationship meant to him.

But for now, her body was urging her to indulge herself. "Why don't you finish your wine," It was time for her fantasy to begin.

"Alright..." Taking her hand, he dipped her fingertips into the deep-crimson wine. Her pulse raced as Arman parted his lips to suck her fingers, one by one before he pulled up her hand and kissed the sensitive inside part of her wrist. Tremors of arousal triggered in her body.

But doubts crowded her mind. This fantasy was a risk and yet, Aleese knew she had to see it through. It was a test. A man that could indulge her fantasies would have the ability to connect to her. It would cut down the layers that Arman had erected and she would know if he really was the man for her. Gathering her strength, she asked, "Do you remember the rules?"

Arman grinned. "You control everything. What would you like me to do?"

"First, I'd like you to go into the bedroom with me."

Arman bowed his head slightly to her. "Your wish is my command, madam." He set down the wine glass and got to his feet. "After you," he said, gesturing towards the bedroom door.

But Aleese wasn't going anywhere yet. She stood and undid her silk robe. Arman's eyes riveted on her as she shrugged it off and let it slide down to the floor. In a sheer black outfit ending at the top of her thighs, Aleese let Arman stare as she reeled him in with her provocative stance. She could feel the heat in her cheeks as his eyes burned into her. Aleese had to remind herself that she was in charge and so, with her head held high, she preceded him into the bedroom, knowing he'd have a tantalizing view of her ass, barely covered by the skimpy lace thong.

* * * *

Ever since he'd seen Aleese at the door, Arman had a hard-on like he couldn't believe. She had bewitched him like no other woman and now she was upping the ante. Whatever she wanted him to do, he'd be willing.

When they entered the bedroom, he was pleased by the ambiance. The tiny gas fireplace lent a warm golden glow to the room as did the scented candles she had placed on the dresser. A strange familiar scent filled the air.

"What is that smell?"

Aleese smiled shyly. "Chocolate candles. What do you think?"

"Nice…" Arman said vaguely, scanning the room for clues. Whatever she had in mind for her fantasy was a mystery. Beyond an ice bucket, a large black box and the jar of body chocolate, there was nothing else here for him to see. "You're keeping me in suspense."

Seating herself on the end of the bed, Aleese crossed her shapely legs. "I like surprising you." With a flick of her finger on the remote, a soft blues tune filled the air. "Slowly take off your uniform. I'd like to sit and watch you strip," she said in a smoky voice.

With that sheer outfit clinging tightly to her breasts, and the exposed half-moons luminous with the candlelight, he desperately wanted to touch her. Delectable treats to be tasted. But he restrained himself, letting his eyes trail down to her toned muscular legs—silky-smooth thighs he'd stroke until she moaned for him to lick her pussy. She was an exotic goddess ready for mortal worship.

He would gladly have whipped his clothes off and took her then and there, but he knew Aleese deserved her fantasy. She hadn't ever asked for anything before and he was willing to provide the performance if that's what she wanted. A challenge, but one he didn't mind indulging her with. In fact, it was exciting to know she wanted to look at his body.

Keeping his distance, he slowly undid the buttons of his jacket, one by one, while he swayed to strains of BB King. He turned away from her as he shrugged the jacket off his shoulders. But he didn't let it drop. Instead, he danced, draping it over his shoulder as he wiggled his hips. Flicking his eyes back, he checked to see what sort of effect his performance was having.

Leaning forward legs uncrossed, watching him, Aleese traced her lower lip with her forefinger as she focused on his ass. Pleased with her reaction, he circled around the room, wondering if she'd notice the significant bulge in his pants.

Tossing his jacket onto the chair, he swiveled around to face her. Loosening his tie, he moved to the rhythm of the music. He was tempted to ditch the strip tease and wrap her wrists in the fabric before he slowly ate her pussy, sucking up every last drop of her nectar. But no, that wouldn't be right. This was her fantasy and he'd stick to the rules. As for the tie, he thought he'd leave it on.

And now the vest. The buttons were smaller, more difficult to open, but between dance moves, he managed to undo them and fling his vest on the chair where it slipped and dropped to the floor. He ignored it and started on his shirt buttons. He wasn't prepared for Aleese entering into his performance. Joining his dance, she decided to help, starting with the lower buttons and when they were all unfastened, she circled around him and tugged on the shirt. He helped with one arm and then the other, but she forced it off, throwing it onto the chair. At the foot of the bed, he stood shirtless, while Aleese hopped back onto the bed, this time sprawled down on her stomach like a kid watching TV.

All right, so she wanted a show—he was up for it. He grinned, thinking his dick sure was, straining to escape the tight confines of his pants, ready for a display. That would turn him on, but no, she wanted this to be slow and sensual and he would be damned if he'd disappoint her.

Arman stepped out of his slip-ons, managing that with some grace. Luckily, he hadn't worn socks. A naked man dancing in socks wouldn't set any woman on fire. Unbuckling his belt he lassoed it in the air before pitching it. By now his stiff rod was exceptionally uncomfortable in the confine of the pants. He had to take them off.

Facing Aleese, he lowered the zipper, and pushed his pants down. When they dropped to the floor, he slowly smiled at Aleese and with a hip movement worthy of any professional stripper, stepped away and started to sway. The music eased into a deliberate beat that stirred his core and set his pulse racing. Wondering if she felt his exhilaration, he searched her face. Cheeks flushed pink and turquoise eyes glimmering like the sea on a sunny day, Aleese had a radiance about her that made him more eager than ever to make love to her.

The boxer-briefs contained an unbelievably ramrod erection that needed to be displayed to his lady. Surely, she'd want to know she was the cause of all of this? Turning away from her he pushed them down over his legs and felt some satisfaction when they hit the hardwood. With his foot he swept them aside and with his tie hanging loosely he pranced over to the end table and dabbed his finger into the chocolate. With a dollop on his finger he encircled the swollen head of his cock with thick chocolate. Strutting back to Aleese, he took a bow, "Did madam like my show?" he asked, rather pleased with himself.

Aleese's eyes were wide, focused on his chocolate-coated cock. "Well done, slave," she murmured, "but you are not finished.

"No?" Arman raised an eyebrow. His mouth twitched in amusement. "What further entertainment does madam desire?"

Aleese uncrossed her legs and stood up. "To the bed, slave." A giggle escaped her lips. "I command you to lie down on your back."

Stretching out on the cover, Arman realized his hard-on was not going down. Her fantasy was intriguing him and obviously thrilling his rod, as well. The women he dated preferred to be submissive partners with the exception of Cisca who had carried out plenty of inspired scenarios of her own. Aleese was a sexual woman, but the start of this little fantasy showed him her potential. Usually, women left it up to him to set the stage for sex, but once again, Aleese proved she was a goddess—one with an active imagination. Intrigued, he waited.

Aleese climbed on the bed and straddled him. "I'll need your hands," she said solemnly.

Agreeably, Arman offered them up. From the black box on the end table, Aleese took out nylon handcuffs. Wrapping each wrist she velcroed the cuffs shut. She then pushed his bound wrists over his head to rest on the pillow. Lifting his head a little, she eased a blindfold over his head and pulled it down over his eyes. The lack of sight intensified his senses. Hearing her rustle around the room Arman was more curious than ever. He waited impatiently for Aleese to return. With the pressure of her weight on the bed, he wondered what she had in mind.

Wispy hair swept down his body—descending from his chest to his groin, caressing his skin and swirling its way back. The next assault was over his nipple. Aroused by the delicate touch of the downy fluff, he longed for more. Would she bring her lips to his very sensitive nipple? He could feel his dick stirring, brushing against her thigh. It would be bliss to lick her skin right now, but the teasing mane departed.

"I don't like the way you're smiling, slave," Aleese said, choking back a nervous giggle.

"I will try not to, madam."

"Don't call me, madam," Aleese ordered sternly. Seriously into her role now, she explained patiently, "I am your mistress and you shall address me accordingly. Do you understand, slave?"

"Of course, madam."

"Stop that, slave!" she said firmly. "I told you, address me as mistress."

Arman felt Aleese push him on his side. Tassels brushed on the curve of his ass. Was that meant to be a whip? He tried hard not to laugh. She swatted him again with the object and sat back. "Say you are sorry, slave."

Arman was amused. If this was her whip, she needed a trade-in. "I'm not sorry for anything."

"You should be, slave," Aleese said sharply and swatted him harder.

"Yes, madam," and couldn't keep the laughter out of his voice. He rolled onto his back.

This time he heard her bounce off the bed, rustle around and return. She sat down against him and forced him to move onto his stomach. He could tell it took an effort for her to push him into this position. He grinned. She was so cute trying this scenario. He was entirely unprepared for what happened next. Something snapped, and his ass cheek felt a sharp sting. Aleese had exchanged the tassel weapon for one with a bit more clout.

"Mistress! I told you," Aleese hissed. "You must address me as mistress!"

Whoa, had she rented a riding crop? He couldn't think of anything else that would have had that sort of wallop. His goddess was getting wicked. He smirked.

"Don't you dare laugh at me!" Aleese finished her words with another sharp snap of the whip.

That one did trigger some pain, Arman thought, but he was a man, after all, and whatever she had in mind for him was only a game, which he'd happily play.

Aleese pushed him down on his back. His poker-stiff dick waited for a little attention from Mistress Aleese. Those sweet lips could suck the swollen head and unleash a flood of cum. Would she? He waited in anticipation for her next move, more stirred up than ever.

Getting on her feet, Aleese wandered away. It sounded like she was digging around in the ice bucket. He waited. Aleese sat on the bed and took her time before he felt the icy chunk pressed to his nipple. A chilling pain yet so intense it thrilled. This was followed by an ice cube on the other nipple. A jolt like electricity struck his core.

Then she soothed him with her tongue, teasing the cool hard peak. It was great. "Suck one, Aleese," he said huskily.

Aleese stopped. "Who's in control here?"

"You, mistress," Arman answered obediently this time. The sheer fabric of the lingerie rubbed against his ready rod. He wanted attention and if it took a bit of submission, what did he or his cock care?

He visualized Aleese in the black outfit. She looked extremely sexy with the low cut of her lingerie partially exposing her beautiful breasts. The red heels had been a turn on, as well. And his rod knew it. If only she'd stroke him. It wasn't fair to push him like this and give so little back. But still, her game was worth playing.

Aleese had stopped giggling. She was Mistress Aleese—a strong dominant female. He'd make an effort to be patient. Those pouty lips could suck him into paradise.

Placated by his reply, Aleese licked him once more and then

gave him a sharp bite followed by a prolonged suck. It made him so hot having his nipple sucked. He could feel his dick go into over-drive. His balls felt tender and swollen. He wanted her more than ever—his special woman.

"I am taking your blindfold off now, slave," Aleese said softly, pulling on the dark cloth.

Arman looked up at Aleese in her frothy black lingerie. She was so beautiful—especially so since she had deprived him of feasting his eyes on her until now. But this change had him very curious. She was up to something.

Aleese sat back facing him and swung up a red stiletto sling back. "Suck my toes, slave," she said throatily. Bringing her foot to his mouth, she waited.

Arman loved her dainty feet and especially her toes. To suck them was no chore—it was a labor of love. His mouth worked the toes exposed by the shoe. He heard Aleese sigh, but he kept on until she withdrew her foot and gave him the other foot. Each toe was given the treatment till her sighs became moans. Aleese withdrew her feet and pushed off each shoe, letting them drop to the floor.

Sitting on the edge of the bed, Aleese said, "You did well, but I have a more difficult assignment for you now. Do you think you can handle it?"

"I will certainly try."

Aleese displayed her pelvis covered by the flimsy material. "Do you see my thong?"

"It is very attractive, mistress."

"Yes, it is. So you must take it off carefully," Aleese said in a hushed voice.

"Would you allow me to remove the cuffs?" Arman focused on the lacy article and what lay beneath. Delicious pussy—so edible.

"Alright…do it."

Arman sat up. The velcroed handcuffs were easy enough to remove. He took hold of her hips and ran his fingers over the thong, brushing velvety smooth skin. With his thumbs he hooked the tiny lacy item and pulled it over her hips.

"Stop, slave. You may take it off, but I will not allow you the use of your hands."

Arman turned his heavy-lidded gaze to her. "Is my mouth

acceptable, mistress?"

Aleese shot him a sultry look. "Yes-ss. Use your mouth."

It was a challenging task, but one he would do willingly. In fact, at this point, Arman hoped she would allow him to eat every bit of her. That thought made him so hot. His stiff cock ached to fill her. Arman was beginning to think this whole fantasy was every bit as fascinating to him as it was excruciatingly painful to his dick. He was as keen as she was to complete this part. Once she was soaking wet, it would be heaven on earth to fuck her. He grinned— if she'd allow it.

His teeth tugged on the thong bringing it to her thighs. Pausing, he licked her inner thighs. It could be the incentive she needed. Hearing Aleese sigh, he lingered—flicking his tongue over her silky skin. He could go on with this indefinitely, but other parts of her needed his attention.

Pulling the garment further down, he continued his exploration to the sensitive area behind her knees. She wriggled with the assault of his licks, her breathing ragged. One last jerk and the thong descended to her ankles. Here, Arman slid his tongue over the inside of her ankle until she squirmed, letting out a low moan. From her dainty feet his tongue wandered on to her toes— in and out until Aleese cried out with the unexpected delight. Leaning on her elbows, Aleese withdrew her foot and kicked off the thong.

His journey not yet over, Arman kissed and licked his way back up her legs, all the while stroking her with his hands. As he neared her inner thighs, Aleese broke away from him.

"Lie down on your back," Aleese whispered.

Arman was hoping for this. Stretched out on the bed, he waited. Straddling him, she brought her pussy close to his mouth and said softly, "Lick me," gripping the headboard for support.

Her heady spicy scent lured him in. This woman was irresistible, Arman thought, cupping her rounded ass with his hands. The tip of his tongue gently caressed her soft folds in search of her swollen nub. At his touch, Aleese moaned. Teasing her rosy clit, Arman licked, enjoying the feel and smell as she thrust her pelvis against his mouth. It didn't matter if it hurt—her pleasure was his sole concern.

Pulling her closer, he let his tongue explore the wet entrance to her pussy. Sticky like honey, but a million times more delicious,

Arman savored Aleese. Retracing his journey, he searched for her clit, his tongue coated with her succulent juice. At the same time his fingers entered the moist opening of her pussy and curling his fingers, he thrust his fingers in and out, hitting her G-spot. Her hot pussy seeped nectar, soaking his hand. Eating her was joy—Arman was consumed by her taste and the feel of her skin. He wanted to make her writhe with pleasure—a goal he relished. The tip of his tongue teased her clit until her ass, slippery with sweat, attempted to twist away. His hands slid on her moist smooth skin, but he gripped her.

"Harder!" Her breathing erratic, Aleese gasped, "I think I'm going to come..."

Holding her tighter, he worked his tongue firmly until she tensed. Suddenly, Aleese jerked uncontrollably and cried out. Without letting up, Arman held contact with his tongue. She screamed. And with each caress of his tongue, she pressed herself against him moaning harder. He was in ecstasy, greedily licking her sweet cum, knowing she was in the last wave of orgasm. Shuddering uncontrollably, a final scream tore out of her before she slumped over the headboard.

Arman watched Aleese slowly lift herself up and sink down on the bed beside him, spent.

"Nice?" he asked casually, studying her lying exhausted beside him.

"Mm-mm!" Aleese murmured her eyes closed.

At this point his dick was begging to drive into her hot wet pussy. "Mistress," Arman asked politely, "is your fantasy over?"

Aleese opened her eyes and grinned mischievously. "No-oo."

Arman frowned. His cock throbbed painfully.

Managing to pull herself up into a sitting position, Aleese gazed into his eyes. "You did admirably, slave, but now I think I'm hungry."

"You want to go out to eat?" Arman asked incredulously. She was torturing him. "Should I get dressed or can we order in?"

"No-oo, neither," Aleese purred. "I think I have something I need to eat right here." She dipped her finger in the chocolate jar and sucked off the decadent syrup. "I love it, but it needs something."

Arman raised an eyebrow. "Oh? I thought it was excellent."

Aleese lifted her sheer black baby doll over her breasts and pulled it over her head, and let it slip to the floor. She was now completely naked and he had a view of her splendid breasts. Her nipples were still hard and Arman longed to make them ache. What he wouldn't give to fondle them, but would she allow it? If her idea was to drive him insane—it was working.

Aleese shoved the tie that hung on his chest aside. "Don't move." Scooping out some chocolate from the jar by the bed, she dabbed his ear lobe, coating it with the dark liquid. Leaning over him, Aleese began to lick up the chocolate while she skimmed his chest lightly with her fingernails. An electric current shot through him. His prick was so swollen, he thought it would burst, yet Aleese's torment continued. She blew lightly into his ear before she thrust the tip of her tongue inside. Arman shuddered with the sensation.

Dipping her finger back into the cocoa syrup, Aleese brought it to his mouth and coated his full lips. Arman's nose registered the rich obsessive scent just before Aleese leaned over and slid the tip of her tongue over his mouth to caress him. The chocolate and the flavor of Aleese mingled and Arman felt as if he had entered nirvana. With his lips parted for her, their tongues played, like two musicians serenading each other—their melodies soothingly sweet yet poignantly intense. He was pulled in, as much as a meteor is pulled into the sun's gravitational force—there was no escape.

When Aleese finally, reluctantly, withdrew, she was breathless. Gazing down at him, she said nothing, but her eyes spoke of the desire she struggled to overcome.

Reaching over to the jar, she once again coated her finger and this time stroked his nipple. Arman bit down a gasp as she manipulated her chocolate-filmed fingers over his hardened tip.

"Sweetheart," he protested, "are you trying to drive me crazy?"

Aleese's turquoise eyes mesmerized him. "And if I did?"

"It would be paradise, as long as you were with me."

"You want me with you?" she asked, pinching his nipples with her fingertips.

Arman groaned with pleasure. Her touch was magic—she had spoiled him for any other woman. "I need you," he said softly before she surrounded his nipple with her mouth.

While she drew it in, a flame blazed in Arman's body. His lust grew with every second she graced him with her lips. As much as he loved what she was doing to him, he wondered when he would be allowed to possess her—hammer his cock into her and make her scream her pleasure.

But Aleese was driven by her own fantasy and wouldn't be stopped. And if she wanted it to be like this, Arman would allow her to use him as her toy. Any other ideas his dick had, would have to go on hold.

After digging into her bottle of delicious decadence, Aleese trailed chocolaty fingers from his taut abs to the base of his dick. When she brushed the back of her hand against his erect member, it moved as if to greet her.

Aleese studied his swollen dick and murmured, "Soon." At least that's what Arman thought she said before she brushed his abs with her tongue and flicked it into the rich brown liquid pooling in his belly button. Her teasing weapon circled before journeying slowly down to his waiting cock.

Aleese lifted her head as she reached back into the jar. Her hungry eyes met his. Surely she'd want to suck his eager dick. Happily, he watched her syrupy fingers approach his swollen member, but instead of touching him there, she ran her thumbs over his inner thighs, her fingertips fondling his tender balls.

"You are an evil woman," he commented, as she took her hand away and bent over to lick the chocolate covering his thighs.

"Oh?" she asked. "Do you want me to stop?"

Arman's lips turned up at the corners. "Evil is good in my books. No, babe, you are definitely on the right track." And then noticing his faux pas, he corrected himself, "I will restrain myself. My apologizes, mistress."

"Too late, slave," Aleese said pertly, picking up the riding crop with her clean hand.

Arman turned on his side. He figured the sooner she got this part over with the faster she'd get to his impatient cock with those long slender fingers of hers. He flinched as she snapped it on his ass. The riding crop was not as stimulating as it had been at the start of her fantasy—mainly because his throbbing rod was at the bursting point.

Happily, she dropped her whip and shoved him down on his back once more. Chocolaty fingers stroked his shaft. "I see you beat me to this spot," she said noticing the brown syrup he had dabbed on his cock after his strip tease, "but, I really like my dessert to have a bit of cream."

Holding his poker-stiff cock with one hand, she licked her way up and down his shaft. Pearly white liquid appeared on the engorged head. Aleese gazed up at him. "See…here it is." She grinned. "*Salud,*" she said, before she took him into her mouth.

The feeling of her lips tightly squeezing was bliss. Arman's cock stirred inside her hot moist mouth. Sitting back against the pillow, his fingers threaded through her fine blonde hair, and with each thrust he could think of nothing but her. Diving deeper into her throat, his dick found a rhythm and Arman entered a state of euphoria.

* * * *

When Aleese heard Arman release a groan she was pleased. Before this, she had only gone down on one boyfriend. It had been a thoroughly unpleasant experience, where she had vacillated between finishing the job and feeling nauseous. But this was different. Everything felt so right. When she'd licked her way up and down his shaft, the smell of citron and soap was enthralling, just like the rest of him. And now, dealing with the mechanics of it, she assumed she was doing it right from his jerks, and the way he gripped her head

"Baby, you want me to come in your mouth?" Arman whispered in his husky voice.

Aleese didn't know. Strangely, the white pearls first released, had tasted wonderful, just like his skin. His cock was a good size and it was pressing into her throat, but the experience was beguiling. With one hand at the base of his shaft, her mouth pressed around his rod and with each thrust gripped harder. Above all, she wanted to give him back some pleasure.

Groaning, his hands tightening on her head, Arman came. When the hot wet stream shot into her mouth, Aleese drank his cum.

Arman sank back into the bed a strange expression on his face.

Sitting up and seeing him like this, Aleese's forehead furrowed. "Was that a disappointment, Arman? You'll need to tell me how to please you better," Aleese said quietly. "I haven't had much experience with going down on a guy."

Reaching out for her, Arman drew her into his arms. "Sweetie, why would you ask that?" He placed a kiss on her cheek. "Everything was perfect."

"And you didn't mind that in my fantasy we didn't..?"

"Fuck?"

Aleese nodded.

"There'll be other times for that." He lifted her chin to him and searched her face. "It was all right for you? You didn't have to swallow it, babe."

"I know. I thought I'd see what it was like."

"And?" Arman asked hesitantly.

"Creamy...almost as good as chocolate."

Arman grinned. "You are too kind, mistress."

"Of course, I may have been overly hasty in saying that. It might require further research."

Arman stroked her cheek. "Why don't we shower and I'll show you how well a slave attends to his mistress." He got up off the bed and gave Aleese his hand. "Come."

Aleese followed Arman into the bathroom, glancing sidelong at his delicious body. This was one of those times when she wished she had a bigger apartment with a luxurious shower—one of those with tiny jets that was capable of massaging every square inch of their bodies.

Adjusting the water temperature, Arman looked around, not put off by the size of the stall or the gentle stream of water that streamed over them.

"Soap?" he asked.

"No, only shower gel. Your choice of cucumber melon or chocolate soufflé."

Arman looked amused. "I can see we'll need to go shopping."

Bringing her hands up to Arman's chest, Aleese circled her fingernails around his nipples. "Not macho enough for you?" Her eyes dropped to his cock which seemed to be rapidly recovering, standing up at half mast. This pleased her. She was definitely having an effect on him. "Well, what about this?" Aleese held up a small bottle of shower gel. It's called Irresistible. It reminds me of you—the way you smell of citron."

"Ah-hh, wise mistress. I use the cologne of the same name, but I admit the shower gel is new to me. I'm afraid I'm a soap type of guy." Arman reached for the bottle and took it from her. "But, I don't mind trying it. No one can say I don't have a sense of adventure. After all, I participated eagerly in your fantasy. Is it over, by the way?"

Aleese nodded. "Part One is."

"I see. I should have anticipated such from my ingenious pixie goddess." He ran his fingers down a tendril of her hair. "I look forward to the rest, then."

"We could do Part Two tonight or I might allow you your turn."

Arman smiled slowly, a glint of mischief in his whiskey eyes. "You are an insatiable goddess. I would definitely be interested in working on one of my fantasies, but first might I assist you?"

Aleese couldn't take her eyes off of Arman. He was so lean and powerful, her pussy started to tingle. "Mm-mm," she said, I could allow you that," reaching for the Irresistible shower gel, "but since this is still my fantasy time…" Squeezing out a few drops of the gel, she brought it to his chest and smoothed it over him. His strong muscles were so touchable. Yet, she had this knot inside her stomach. Fear, perhaps. What she felt for Arman was way beyond the physical. She was more convinced than ever that she was in love and with that came vulnerability.

Arman studied her. "So serious, mistress. Are you worried I won't be able to handle the rest of your fantasy? Let me assure you, I have no problem with Part Two." He glanced at the shower gels. "Hm-mm," he said, picking up a shower gel, "I am one hundred per cent sure this is your favorite," pouring a dollop of chocolate soufflé on the palm of his hand. "May I?"

Nodding her head, Aleese stood still while he cupped one breast and with the other smoothed on the chocolate shower gel. Her body trembled from his contact. His hands were magic and her nipple perked to his tender touch. At this point, she didn't care if this was part of her fantasy or his. She delighted in his hands sliding over her body, but she couldn't stop thinking. Was this only a fling for him? While Arman stroked the gel over her belly, Aleese tried to read his expression. Was it possible he could be in love with her? How could she tell?

"Turn, sweetheart."

Frustrated with the uncertainty of her situation, she frowned.

Misunderstanding, Arman lightly kissed her lips. "Don't be

embarrassed. Your ass is beautiful." Stepping behind her, Arman rubbed the gel over her cheeks. "I could stare at it all day but," he laughed, "I think I'd rather touch it."

Her legs were like jelly—that was the effect he had on her, especially as he stroked her inner thighs. Looking at his powerful body, Aleese wasn't sure how to tell him about the next part of her fantasy. It wasn't a difficult thing for him, but for her to ask put her in a sticky situation. It was her dream to be carried to bed by a strong sexy guy—and that man was Arman. She remembered how he had done it at his condo and how even though she had been angry, he'd made her aware of how much a man he was. But if she asked, he might think she was being ridiculously romantic. Maybe it was a stupid idea.

"What is it, sweetheart? Am I doing this wrong?" Arman said sliding his fingers over the silky folds.

"No, it feels good." Aleese pulled herself together and dropped some shower gel in her hands and brought them to his abs. "Let me put some on you." That lean lanky form standing there before her was perfect. Touching him gave her such a rush that for a moment, she forgot all her doubts and fears. Slowly, she explored him, trailing her fingertips lower past his rod. Fondling his balls gently, she came back to his shaft and slid them up to the head and down again. She could feel his rod growing with each stroke.

"Tell me about the next part of your fantasy, babe."

"Promise you won't laugh?"

Arman wrapped his arms around her. "You can trust me. I will try to accommodate you, if it's possible."

"It is possible, Arman, but you might think I'm being silly."

Arman pulled them both into the shower's gentle spray. The water rinsed away the scented gels and with one hand he grabbed a towel from the rack and dried off Aleese. When she was completely dry, he brought the towel around her and tucked it in above her breasts. Taking a second towel he dried himself off and placed it around his waist. "Come, baby, I think we should talk."

Aleese felt nervous. He was a very sexual man and if she told him about this fantasy, he might be disappointed in her. When he led her back into the bedroom, he drew her down beside him on the edge of the bed.

Arman's eyes reflected amber as he gazed intently at her. "I won't laugh and I will take your fantasy seriously. Now tell me what it is."

Turning to him, Aleese started, "I wanted you to carry me to bed and make love to me but," she glanced at the bed, "since we are here already, I guess we could try out your fantasy."

"Well," Arman said slowly, "that might be a problem." He flicked his eyes on the jar of body chocolate. "Could I have another taste of that chocolate?"

Aleese was puzzled. He was so blasé about the whole thing. What was wrong with him? Picking up the jar she passed it to him.

But instead of digging into it, Arman asked, "Would you mind giving me some chocolate?"

Passing him a curious glance, Aleese stuck her finger into the chocolate and brought her finger up to his mouth.

Arman sucked the chocolate from her finger, smiled and said, "How about another."

The pressure of his lips surrounding her finger set off a series of fireworks in her body—her cheeks flushed with heat, her nipples flamed and her pussy sparked. This man had the power to stir her juices with one simple act. Propelled into seventh heaven, she dipped her finger in once more, but this time she felt something inside the jar besides chocolate.

Aleese pulled it out. "What's this?" she said holding up a chocolate-covered key.

Arman drew his feet up and lay down on the bed. Stretching out, he closed his eyes and yawned. "You know, babe, I'm really tired."

Wiping the key with a tissue, she looked at it again. What was it for? When she swung about to question him further, his breathing had become deeper and his head had turned away. "Arman?" she asked, lightly shaking his shoulder.

There would be no answers tonight—Arman was fast asleep.

12

A key covered in body-chocolate.

When she awoke, this was the only thing on Aleese's mind. She flicked her gaze to the golden key on the end table.

Maddening. That's what it was. Arman had fallen asleep without telling her what it was for. She smiled. Of course, she couldn't blame him much. His tongue had experienced an unbelievable workout.

Mouth-watering smells of breakfast wafted in the air. Aleese sat up. This was an unexpected pleasure. Who would have thought a man who could fire a flame in her body could also heat up delicious morsels in the kitchen?

Excited to see Arman again after her fantasy night, she padded over to the dresser and pulled out a yellow bra with a pushup that gave her an enticing cleavage—one that Arman would be sure to notice. The matching low-cut panties would be a bonus.

Through the window, the day looked warm and sunny. Everything was almost perfect. Almost, but not quite. Aleese frowned. If only she knew what Arman felt for her? She bit her lip. If he couldn't return her love, should she continue to see him? A man like him could have any number of Shannas. And with his high sex drive, Arman would find it difficult to throw them out of bed. On the other hand, she couldn't do that—a collection of boyfriends wouldn't be right for her. Aleese already knew who she wanted. But if he dated other women, she'd be forced to break up with him. It would drive a knife through her heart if she knew he was with another woman.

Seeing her puffy reflection in the mirror, she zipped into the bathroom, and splashed some water on her face before she brushed on mascara. Finishing off with a touch of lip gloss, she padded back into the bedroom and donned shorts and a t-shirt, before she headed out to the kitchen to see Arman.

Bare muscular thighs and powerful calves. He was shirtless. Boxer-briefs covered a firm ass. For a moment, Aleese stood still, mesmerized by the sight of him—a Greek god would have envied a body as fine as his.

Arman was frying an omelet and her stomach responded to the food as vigorously as her pussy did to the man. "Good morning," she said softly.

Swinging around, his eyes took her in. "Any morning is good when I can see you. Everything is ready if you want to grab the glasses. We'll eat out on your balcony."

She smiled. "You do like balconies, don't you?"

"Especially if I get to eat something I like," Arman said with a grin.

Aleese's mouth curled down at the corners. "I'm afraid this one is too small for anything but breakfast."

"Maybe in the Bahamas…"

Aleese frowned. He still hadn't mentioned love—only good times. It was true that Puerto Rico had been wonderful, but was their relationship only about sex? No matter what happened, she needed to know.

Arman gave her a curious look. "You haven't changed your mind?" he asked, sliding the balcony door open.

"About?" Aleese asked distractedly.

"Going to New York."

"If it's in the summer, but, Arman, we really should…"

"I see what you mean," he said, setting the plates down on the tiny round table. "Very tiny, but it will do."

"What's this?" Aleese lifted the glass filled with the bubbly-orange liquid. She glanced at Arman who had taken the chair beside her.

"I brought some champagne and when I saw you had orange juice, I thought you might like a celebratory drink."

"What are we celebrating?" Aleese asked curiously.

"Your fantasy." Arman placed his finger on her lips. "It was very arousing. *Salud*," he said, clicking his glass to hers.

"*Salud*," Aleese said trying not to sound disappointed. She had really wanted him to say something romantic. It was wonderful he wanted to give her pleasure, but it bothered her he said nothing about love or commitment. Bravely, she put those thoughts aside and said, "It was fantastic, Arman, but what about yours?"

"We'll get to it." He forked up a portion of omelet and brought it to his lips.

Aleese, having sampled her omelet, complimented him, "This is delicious, Arman. You never told me you could cook."

"There are many things I haven't told you."

"Things I should know?" Aleese probed.

"If you're patient you'll find some out today." Arman cut into his omelet.

"Your fantasy, you mean?"

His eyes wandered from her face to her shorts and t-shirt. "You look good like that. Did I ever tell you your eyes are fascinating?"

Aleese gave him a look. "Seems to me your attention is usually focused on the curves of my derrière."

"And such a nice one it is." Arman's lips curved upwards. "But it was negligent of me to not tell you how lovely your eyes are, and those kissable lips of yours are the subject of my dreams."

"Dreams?" Aleese grinned. "You mean they set off your masturbation fantasies?"

"Only a small part. I like to imagine a whole scenario. And you?"

Aleese flushed, thinking of how Arman had been the subject of numerous fantasies. "Yes, I have a few scenarios in different settings." Aleese sipped her drink and fantasized.

"Which involve?"

Aleese hesitated. "There are a lot, but if you really want to know…"

"I do."

"The beach, a restaurant, a car, a hot tub…"

"Would you like to do one? I mean, if you were in that location, would you tell me what it was?"

"I might." She dug into the last bit of her breakfast. "Arman, there was something I needed to ask you."

"Yes?"

Visions of his chocolate-covered cock appeared before her eyes. "Last night, you gave me that jar of body butter."

"Which we finished." Arman took up her hand and rubbed her palm. "Did you like it?"

Aleese trembled at his touch—her nipples perked longing for his hands to excite them.

"Aleese? Did you like it?"

His rod had tasted surprisingly good. "You know how much I

love chocolate. Did you like it?"

Arman laughed. "I think you got to eat the major portion. Not much left for me to sample except what was on your sweet lips and fingertip. But, I'm not complaining, what I got to eat was irresistible."

Aleese flushed at the thought of his tongue on her tingling pussy. "Arman, there is something that you didn't explain. You fell asleep before telling me about the key in the chocolate jar. What is it for?"

Arman sat back in his chair and gazed at her. "I think it would be best if you saw for yourself."

"We're driving somewhere?" Her buff boyfriend in boxer-briefs was eye-candy—delectably sweet like chocolate but hardly dressed for a drive.

"Soon."

* * * *

Arman took his eyes off the road to glance sidelong at Aleese's slim hand sliding along his leg. She was playing him like a violin—her fingers gliding over his inner thigh. He could feel his erection growing.

"So tell me, Arman."

"About?" he asked grinning.

Aleese took her hand away from his thigh.

Arman felt his cock stir. "You are playing hard ball, babe. You know how I love," he said stroking her hand, "this little hand on me."

"Then you'll have to tell me about the key, won't you?"

"Be patient, babe.

Slowing down, he pulled into a circular driveway. From the corner of his eye, he watched Aleese. She was sitting more erect, looking at the attractive white condominium before them.

The tree-lined road led to an underground parking lot. At the gate, he pressed a security key. The steel door rose and he drove in. After parking at a spot close to the stairs, he grabbed his carry-on, got out and walked around to open the door for Aleese.

Perplexed, she asked, "Why are we here, Arman?"

Placing his hand at the small of her back, he led her to the stairs. "Chill."

"But…"

Arman took her hand and she went with him up the stairs to an elevator. He pressed the button and it opened. "All your questions will be answered in a moment."

Inside, he put his finger on twelve and the elevator began its ascent. The doors opened to a hallway tiled in white marble. Taking her hand, Arman steered her to the last door.

"Do want to open it?" Arman asked.

"The gold key," Aleese said slowly in realization. Digging into her purse she pulled it out and stuck it in the keyhole. With a turn the door clicked. She swung it open. "What is this place, Arman?"

Sweeping a startled Aleese in his arms, he kicked the door open wider and carried her inside. Setting her down, he wrapped his arms around her. "It's ours," he said softly, before kissing her.

Her lips were lusciously soft and she tasted sweeter than honey. His kiss lingered, searching for something indefinable while his tongue reveled in her flavor. Deeply, he drove into her mouth, feeling the electricity between them, connecting their minds with their bodies. Their kiss would last forever, if he had the choice.

Her mouth deliciously bruised—Aleese broke away from his arms. "Ours," she repeated slowly. Her eyes shot to the vaulted cathedral ceiling. Light poured in from the skylight above on the white stuccoed walls. A leather chair stood at one end of the room near the fireplace, but apart from that, the room was void of furniture. "What do you mean?" she asked hesitantly, in an attempt to understand.

Arman grabbed her hand and swung her around in a dance move. "I bought the condo and I want you to move in here with me. There's plenty of room for your furniture—for all your things. Hope you don't mind the bed and the chair, but let me show you." Taking her elbow, he steered her by a kitchen with an island counter and bar seats to a doorway which she assumed was the bedroom. "What do you think?" he asked, gesturing to the four-poster king-sized bed, the Jacuzzi and the fireplace in the corner near the balcony doors.

"It's beautiful." She tilted her head up to look in the eyes. "Did you mean it? You really want me to live with you?"

"You are the woman for me, goddess." He ran his finger down her cheek. "And if you want it legal, I think I could be persuaded."

"Oh?" she said, a mischievous glint in her ocean-blue eyes. She stepped away from him and lifted her t-shirt, drawing it over her head and letting it fall to the floor. Giving him a sultry look she undid the snaps of her shorts and tugged them off her hips till they slipped down, joining her top. "Who says I want to?" Aleese sauntered to the hot tub and turned it on.

Arman's dick stood at attention as he watched her bend down, lacy panties barely covering her rounded cheeks. Aleese was so beautiful his brain boggled. All he could think about was which would she do first—unfasten her bra to display her fabulous breasts or pull off her panties to show off her curvaceous cheeks?

Turned away from him, she reached behind her to undo the hooks on her bra. Shrugging the garment off, she then pushed down her thong. Arman froze mesmerized, as she slipped out of her sandals and stepped into the bubbling tub. Standing nude in the steamy water, she was as lovely as the sirens luring sailors to their deaths, especially when she swiveled around to beckon him to come to her.

Arman made sure he took his clothes off slowly—his t-shirt and his shorts followed by his boxer briefs. He didn't dance this time, but he made sure her eyes were riveted on him. Before he went to her, he dug out a small narrow object wrapped in tissue from his carry-on.

When he stepped into the tub, Aleese had already sunk deep into the bubbling water. The water covered most of her. She stared at him in a silent challenge.

He placed the parcel on the ledge and wasting no time, he pulled her on top of his lap. "Lean back against me, sweetheart," he said in his husky voice.

"Arman?"

"Yes, babe?"

"Is that for me?" Aleese asked breathlessly.

"It is. I thought we should try my fantasy."

"And what exactly did you want me to do?"

Arman wrapped his arms around her and leaned into her ear. "I'd like to see you masturbate and I'll help."

"Here?"

"If you'd like to."

"It's wonderful in here," Aleese said slowly. "You know how

water makes me feel so good, don't you? I love the jets massaging my body and if I open my legs, I feel the most delicious sensation." She tilted her head to Arman. "Should I unwrap it?"

Arman nodded and handed it to her. It was a pleasure to watch her. Aleese took a child's joy in unraveling the paper to get to the object beneath. Penis-shaped but narrow, pink and smooth, it curved up on the end. "Is it waterproof, Arman?" she asked, turning it on. The vibrator hummed strongly as if in answer.

"Go ahead, goddess. It's safe and sure to please." He handed her a bottle. "Coat it first."

* * * *

The water bubbled high over Aleese's breasts. She felt totally relaxed sitting on Arman with the jets shooting over her. And she felt so happy. Arman really did love her. He must, even though he hadn't said so. Looking around the bedroom, she couldn't have chosen a better place herself. It was spacious with bay windows and a balcony overlooking a park. She eyed the balcony—so similar to the one in San Juan. Nothing had been more exciting to her than that.

Beneath her, Aleese felt the hardness of Arman's cock. Tingles in her pussy made her aware of how much she wanted him inside her, but it was his turn for a fantasy and she'd be true to her word. Closing her eyes she took the vibrator and placed it on her clit. With her other hand she caressed her nipple before Arman's large hand came up to cup her breast. She let her hand drop to grip his thigh in order to stabilize her in the rushing water. It wasn't difficult for her to start imagining as she always did when she masturbated.

Her thoughts went back to the balcony in San Juan—how Arman had dropped to his knees, slid his hands up her legs and kissed every sensitive area along the way until he reached her hot wet pussy. There, with the rain splattering her body, his velvety tongue had licked her soft folds and teased her clit until she came in a tremendous orgasm. She had never imagined doing anything like that before and now, when she let the vibrator tickle her clit, she played out that scenario while Arman's hand smoothed over her breast.

The vibes were strong. She squirmed as the vibrator's silky

surface pulsed her clit. With Arman's fingers kneading her nipple and his tongue tracing the curves and flicking into the opening of her ear, she trembled in arousal. The warm breath on her neck made her nipples swell into peaks. Curling into his body, she arched her back to expose her throat for his kisses all the while pushing the vibrator harder.

But it was Arman who sent her soaring into an ecstatic space— nibbles on the curve of her neck while his hands stroked her breasts.

Aleese visualized him entering. The length of the vibrator was against her folds, the tip in the opening of her vaginal lips. Rapidly, she moved the tantalizing machine back and forth, her hand aching and tired until the sensation surged to a new precipice. She shuddered, groaning as she hurdled over passion's cliff. Crying out again, she came, her body jerking erratically in orgasm. It was so intense, it wouldn't stop. Gyrating frantically for an endless minute, she finally sank back exhausted. It took extreme effort to shut off the vibrator.

"Is that what you wanted?" she asked weakly.

"Only part of it," Arman said, pulling her up. Grabbing a towel he wrapped it around her before carrying her over to the bed and placing her on top.

"I'm still wet," Aleese cautioned.

Arman growled hoarsely, "Get on your hands and knees."

Slippery from her orgasm, Arman's swollen cock easily entered her from behind. She squeezed him tightly, holding him inside as he rammed her like no one had ever done before. Each thrust propelled her forward, but she firmly situated herself on the bed determined to receive his powerful attack. Fingers slid on her clit rhythmically. Euphoria as never before, yet it was the battering of her G-spot which ignited sky rockets into other realms.

The animal in her arched to his slick wet body wanting more and more. The savage pounding inside her pussy along with the intense pleasure forced a primal scream from somewhere deep inside her—an agonizing cry that went on, distant in her ears until she felt herself gripped in a corset of pain. Shuddering, she came— and so did he. Arman's cum flooded into her hot juices. Spent and satiated, Aleese fell forward with Arman dropping down beside her. Her eyes closed. Her tiger clutched her tightly to him, his breath on her neck.

"Was there more to this fantasy?"

"Yes-ss, babe, but I'll need a minute."

With an effort, she pushed herself about to face him. "A minute, eh?"

Arman grinned. "Okay...two minutes, goddess."

Stroking his damp cheek, Aleese murmured, "That was one powerful fantasy. I think you had an urge to dominate me, mm-mm?"

"You happy with that?"

"For a moment there, I thought I'd end up in the next condo."

Arman's finger traced her lips. "We. Let me remind you that those strong pussy muscles held me in a vice-grip."

She kissed his finger. "I guess we really are going places together."

"Yes, I hope so." Arman paused and wrapped his arms around her. "I wasn't sure if you'd be okay with this, but I accepted an invitation for us. My parents' place tonight."

Aleese bolted upright. "You told them about me?"

"I said I'd be bringing home the most beautiful woman in the world."

"You are so sweet, Arman. Do you think they'll like me?"

Arman's eyes twinkled. "What's not to like—you're smart, lovely and funny."

"Your mother will want a little more for her son."

"You cook?"

Aleese nodded.

"All set then."

"My parents will be a harder sell." Aleese brushed her hair away from her eyes. "They thought I'd marry Mr. Engineer."

"Not a problem. I've been trained to handle difficult situations, remember? Why don't we bring them over to my parents? They ought to know what their daughter's up to, don't you think?"

With an adoring gaze, Aleese said, "My mom will think you're cute."

"At least we'll have her on our team." Arman gave her a rakish look. "By the way, I think my two minutes are up."

Aleese raised an eyebrow. "There are some things we haven't talked about yet." She ran her fingernails down his chest, "Maybe if you answer all my questions," she brought her mouth to his ear, feathering the tip of her tongue down to his lobe, and whispered, "we might complete your fantasy."

With a groan, Arman lifted her on top of him. "Sure thing, goddess, but why don't we work on that fantasy first and then I'll answer your questions." He brought her closer and licked the hollow of her throat while his hands slid down her back, cupping the cheeks of her ass.

A sigh escaped her lips. Briefly she allowed him to continue before pulling back. He was sinfully delicious like chocolate. She needed to think clearly, but Aleese couldn't resist nibbling his bottom lip slowly before sliding her tongue over the surface of his mouth.

Aroused by her touch, Arman pressed his lips against her, but again, she retreated a fraction, tantalizing him with her nearness, yet too far out of reach for him to kiss her back.

Aleese slid her body against his wet body. Musk and soap with a hint of citron. A man couldn't smell better than this.

* * * *

Massaging the firm cheeks of Aleese's ass excited Arman. He would set his tongue to work to flame her passion. If she wanted to tease him with her lips he would make her go crazy. Taking up her arm, he licked the inside of her elbow with tiny butterfly licks. He heard Aleese's quick intake of breath as he pressed his tongue on the same spot repeatedly. With his hand, he held her arm in place, his lips tightly pressed to her skin, making escape impossible. When she moaned, Arman sucked harder. He could feel Aleese wrap her legs around his. Her hands raked his back, her fingernails digging in. The pain aroused him.

"Get on top of me, goddess," Arman said, his cock, poker-stiff, wanting to be inside her tight pussy.

Without hesitation, Aleese straddled him, slowly lowering herself down on his firm, thick member. And then she cat-stretched over him.

Arman groaned with the contact. Her brilliant blue pools gleamed in the morning light—changeable like the Caribbean. He wanted to touch every part of her. Her lovely breasts with their rosy-tipped nipples thrust forward as she moved towards him. He captured a breast and brought his mouth to the hardened peak sucking fiercely. Aleese gasped. Easing his pressure, he licked her gently. She let him and then pulled away, rocking back to an upright position. Looking down at him, she said, "I can't move in here with you."

Arman couldn't believe his ears. "Why?" he asked, astonished.

Not answering, she pushed against him while teasing his lips with her tongue—his dick on the receiving end of a pelvic squeeze. Aleese sat up. "How do you feel about me?"

Arman groaned with the pressure. She was so hot and wet. An irresistible woman that brought him to paradise and back whenever she wanted. She pushed every button he had and others he never knew existed. Why was she asking insane questions? He jerked his cock up into her, driving harder as she rocked back and forth. Tugging her head down to his mouth, he kissed her deeply.

Aleese pulled away. "Tell me, Arman."

What the hell was she talking about? Didn't she know she was incredible? "I'm crazy about you, Aleese!" Arman snapped.

Aleese gripped his arms. "Inside…emotionally?"

"Baby, you know," he murmured hoarsely.

Aleese slouched back before she flung herself down rubbing her clit on him once more. "Tell me!"

"I love you!" he shouted, jerking inside her.

Aleese smiled happily.

"Your turn!" He slapped her ass. "Now, you say it."

Aleese moaned.

Arman smacked her cheeks again. "Say it!"

Jolting violently, Aleese screamed out—pleasure wiring her body. Tremors took over. "Omigod, I love…you!"

Arman shot his hot liquid into her. Wrapping his arms around her, he pulled her close as she sank into his embrace. He growled, "My irresistible goddess. Will you move in with me now?"

"Mm-mm, I will," Aleese purred.

He kissed her soft lips tenderly. "I really do love you." His eyes met hers. "Never ever doubt it."

*****

www.AnastasiaAmor.com
Anastasia.Amor@hotmail.com
www.facebook.com/Anastasia.Amor.author

http://anastasiaamor1.blogspot.ca

ACKNOWLEDGEMENTS

Thank you, Barbara, for suggesting I write an erotic novel. It was a new exciting challenge. And many thanks to Jane and Bruce. I appreciate all of you for your friendship and support.

By ANASTASIA AMOR

ADIE STURM MYSTERIES

Corpse for Cozumel
Days of the Dead
The Curse of the Carnaval
Dead Delicious

PARANORMAL FANTASY SERIES
Havana Heat

EROTIC ROMANCE
Exploring Irresistible

ABOUT THE AUTHOR

OKTOBERFEST WOMAN OF THE YEAR FINALIST and EPIC AWARD NOMINEE, ANASTASIA AMOR is a university psychology and education graduate. She is the proud mother of two, a pet-mom and a teacher. She also speaks German and is learning Spanish. Art and writing are her passions but she loves to dance and is a known chocoholic.

Praise for Anastasia Amor

HAVANA HEAT**...a paranormal fantasy romance...**5 stars!
"Havana Heat is a sensory experience. Fast paced and drop dead sexy..."—*Natalie G. Owens*, author of ***An Eternity of Roses***

"Twists and turns in this tropical romance make it a paranormal reading adventure that will keep you on your toes until the last word!"—*Barbara Huffert*, author of ***Linked***

THE CURSE OF THE CARNAVAL: ADIE STURM MYSTERY— Epic Nominee 2011

"Adie's back and it's hotter than ever, way hotter. And far more dangerous....Thanks for the escape, Ms. Amor."—*ChrisChat Reviews*

A CORPSE FOR COZUMEL: ADIE STURM MYSTERY

"...hot sexy men... thrilling suspense... You won't guess who the killer is until it's too late." —*Night Owl Romance Reviews*

DAYS OF THE DEAD: ADIE STURM MYSTERY

4 Books! "...You never can tell just what will crop up...a fun read, and will be very welcomed by fans of the series."—*LongAndShort Reviews*

DEAD DELICIOUS—Highly Recommended!
"Anastasia Amor is truly the queen of steamy mysteries." — *Natalie G. Owens, An Eternity of Roses.*

www.ingramcontent.com/pod-product-compliance
Lightning Source LLC
Chambersburg PA
CBHW060811250626
47162CB00005B/1737